A*hole

Hilton Obenzinger

A * hole

Hilton Obenzinger

Soft Skull Press * 2004
Brooklyn, NY

A*hole
ISBN: 1-932360-46-8
©2004 by Hilton Obenzinger

Cover Design by Charles Orr
ShortLit Series Design by David Janik and Charles Orr

Published by Soft Skull Press * www.softskull.com
Distributed by Publishers Group West * www.pgw.com

Printed in Canada

Cataloging in Publication information for this book is
available from the Library of Congress

I am grateful to Robert Harrison for his insights on Dante, and to Paul Auster, Stephen Vincent, and Mark Williams for editorial suggestions and support. Also, I would like to thank my students Simonette Jones, Kumar Narayanan, and Rachel Turow for their ideas, and Yolanda Ochoa for allowing me to adapt her account of the confrontation in Robinson Mays in L.A.

Chapter One appeared in *FACTURE 2,* 2001;
Chapter Three appeared in *Jacket Magazine*, August 2002,
both in earlier versions.

ONE

Sinking

My parents became worried when I refused to go outside, so I didn't tell them for a long time that the reason I wouldn't go to school or even out on the street was because I was sinking.

When I walked outside that day and took my very first step out of the door of our building I sank into the sidewalk. I just sank a tiny bit, maybe a hair, but I felt it for sure, yet when I picked up my foot there was no footprint left behind like when you walk on Jones Beach, and the sidewalk just covered itself back over where my foot had been.

I went to school the first day I began to sink, and with every step I could feel that I was sinking deeper and deeper, and I was sure people would notice, the doorman would complain about the footprints ruining the sidewalk in front of the building, though he didn't seem to mind or notice, the other kids would yell and scream, or for sure the teachers would rub their chins and call my parents, but no one could see it or maybe no one cared. By the time I got home I could barely see the tops of my Reeboks, it was like walking through an inch or two of snow, so I knew it was getting serious.

When I got inside the school building the sinking stopped, and the same thing happened when I got back to the lobby of our our apartment building, and I didn't sink through the floor of our apartment either. Only when I was outside on the sidewalk or on the street did it happen. The next day I tried again, and I began to sink the second I stood out on the pavement, and I raced back up to the apartment, and decided I would never step outside again or else who knew how much I might sink the next time, up to my knees, up to my neck, and I didn't want to find out, it was too scary.

At first my parents thought I was trying to play hooky, but I told them school was OK just so long as it came to me but that I wouldn't go to it, and they pleaded with me to tell them what was wrong, were the kids mean, and then they thought I was just being stubborn and I just wanted to cut school, but after I was willing to get spanked or yelled at just so I wouldn't have to step outside they really began to worry. I was sorry to make them so upset, and I really meant it, and I told them I was sorry, but I wasn't crazy enough to go outside and get swallowed up.

Finally, I had to explain to them what was happening, that I was sinking into the ground. At first they looked surprised, with a strange, curious look, but then they said they understood, although all that meant was that instead of yelling at me they began to whisper to each other. After whispering awhile they told me that I better see a doctor in order to help me, that maybe I could take some medicine which would stop me from sinking, some kind of "anti-quicksand" pill. I told them there wasn't any quicksand, that it was still solid sidewalk in Manhattan, but that for some reason I was able to pass right through all the pebbles and molecules and stuff, or maybe they passed through me, and I didn't know why. So they just called it "anti-sinking" medicine instead, and they explained that doctors knew how to cure the problem if I would just go visit one.

But how could I go out to visit a doctor if I might slip deep under the ground with my very first step? I said the doctor was OK, but only if he came to the apartment. No way was I going to walk outside. But they argued and argued and told me not to worry and that they would each hold me by the hand and if I sank they would hold me up long enough to get me into a cab waiting right outside the door. So finally I agreed.

I put on a pair of new Nikes—they said new shoes might help—and we took the elevator down. When we reached the lobby I couldn't take it anymore and tried to go back into the elevator but they grabbed my arms and told me not to worry, they were with me and would protect me. But I knew otherwise, I knew that once you start to sink through the earth you never stop. It's one of those things that you feel inside you without knowing why or how, just that it's true.

They said I had to go. The doorman held the door open, the taxi driver stood next to his cab, and Mom and Dad stepped right outside, reached in for my hands, and pulled me through.

The first step I took I sank up to my ankles. They all stared in amazement. The doorman's eyes bugged out like one of the Three Stooges; the taxi driver ran behind the double-parked cab, hoping the trunk would protect him; all four of them shouted in alarm, and Mom and Dad grabbed my hands even tighter. I kept my other foot back on the doorsill; then I took the next step.

In an instant I began to sink more than ever, up to my knees, sliding down into the sidewalk like it was warm butter, and this time I kept dropping, until the sidewalk was up to my chin, my hands over my head. Mom and Dad screamed but held on even as I sank over my head, and they held on to my fingertips as I reached up over my head until they couldn't hold on any longer. My fingertips slipped beneath the concrete, but for Mom and Dad the concrete was still hard, so they had to let go when their own knuckles scrapped against the ground.

Then I was sliding through dirt and darkness all alone, their screams growing fainter the deeper I plunged.

Falling

I was in the middle of my life and relatively comfortable, except for my son. In high school he was troubled, filled with fear, facing a kind of mental horror every day. When he entered the hospital, they took his belt and shoe laces. Maybe there was something I had done; maybe something in my past was screwing him up, some bad influence. Or perhaps there was something I should have done, some obvious sin of omission. You get into this kind of state when your kid's in trouble, and I think that's how my own problems began.

The doctors call it benign positional vertigo. Little crystals in your inner ear slip from one place to another—most of the time doctors don't know why—and the world starts spinning or your equilibrium goes to the dogs. I learned to live with it, just as I learned to live with my other troubles, even though walking a straight line can be quite a chore. From time to time I carry a cane just to keep from keeling over.

That night I was making my way along a San Francisco street, deep in thought, worrying about my son, when the vertigo took hold with such power that I felt as though an earthquake had struck. The ground heaved up and down like ocean swells, although no one else on the street seemed alarmed and the cars calmly passed each other without swerving. I, however, reeled and stumbled, my cane snapped in two and I lost my footing, hurtling forward with such tremendous force that I thought I was going to smash my jaw on the concrete. I put my arms out to break the fall, dropping the large briefcase I ordinarily carry with me. Up to now I imagined I was simply tossed around by the vertigo, but then things got very strange; instead of hitting the pavement, I kept on falling, never hitting the ground.

I never did reach the ground, although the sidewalk seemed very much where it belonged. It's just that I kept on falling, and there was a great distance to go before I would slam into the pavement. I noticed that my briefcase—filled with papers and books and other things important to a writer—was also tumbling down alongside me. The flap had opened up, and all sorts of junk began to fall out, seeming to race ahead, things I hadn't realized that I was carrying or even could carry: dreams, memories, old address books, frying pans, tax returns, regrets, and more. I expected an elephant or a house to fly out. Why not? Still, I admit I was alarmed when a white-shingled cottage did tumble out, defying gravity.

I certainly had wandered off from the straight and narrow. It was one of those typical stucco houses in San Francisco, and only the shingles made it stand out in any way—that and, of course, the fact that it had fallen from my briefcase. I assured myself that this was some kind of delusion, but I went ahead and knocked, and when no one answered, I tried the door. It was open, and I stepped in. The house seemed to be composed of the bits and pieces of my life jumbled up with stuff that belonged to other people—torn books, old jokes, knickknacks, legends. I couldn't tell the evidence of my own journey through life from the airplane tickets and birth announcements of others, all scattered in the halls, thrown on the livingroom floor, dangling from magnets on the refrigerator door. I ran around trying to put it all together, all the fragments and scraps, the unpaid bills, the sex fantasies, and sorrows, yanking out the stuff I knew was mine, trying to piece together who I was or thought I was—or at least who I could be—but nothing seemed to match, nothing seemed to make sense.

I began to panic. Could it be I was so addled that I had actually walked into some stranger's house on the street? I didn't break, but I did enter, so I decided I had better make my way out before the cops sped to the scene. I stepped through the debris cluttering the floor and fled out the door.

As soon as I walked into the street, I started to fall again, the sidewalk receding, seeming to drop away from me at a fantastic pace as I tumbled down. Why did this happen? Why did I keep falling yet never seemed to touch bottom? This was not some nihilist philosophy or a fashionable attitude that life is merely channel surfing. No, this was a terrible confusion, vertigo worse than I had ever experienced. I had entered a mental state no Wittgenstein or Freud or even Walt Disney knew how to deal with.

While the crystals in my inner ear may have slipped, the crystals in my inner soul seemed to have wandered off altogether.

The end is near

I shook the rain from my hat
    and walked into the room.
        Nobody said a word.

            Originally every city was holy, but now
            only the one that I am about to leave is holy.

HILTON OBENZINGER

Reader, I have returned from the dead to tell you what I have seen, although I may have only been locked in a closet with Patty Hearst.

Do not be afraid.

Call me Isaac.

It stood there, like a holstered gun, ready to spring into action with a quick, cold click, its skeleton lofting upward to form a great hood overhead, arching sleek black fabric skyward with disarming irony, all at the end of nothing more than a common walking stick. Then it began to rain.

Who is, who was, who is to be.

Whoosh.

My eyes opened, but I could see nothing.
    My eyes closed, and everything became clear.
My dream ended, and I became confused.
    My dream resumed, and my eyes opened.

The end is

A thick shield of smoke
hangs over the city, the pall protecting it
from the gaze
of the bombardier

Delete.

Nobody said a word. Nobody had to.
The body sprawled across the floor, rigid.

The Last Supper

The last straw

The last dance

The last chance

The last will be first

Nothing lasts

My dream resumed, and nobody said a word.

No body

Only the one I am about to leave

Satan's Asshole

"See, to get to heaven you got to go to hell, the very bottom of hell, and there's Satan, and he's there with his three mouths chewing on the world's biggest sinners, and what you got to do is crawl into Satan's asshole. That's right, the way to get to heaven is right through Satan's asshole! Can you believe it?"

I eyed the gunman with a blank stare.

"Do you think I'm kidding or something, motherfucker?" he shouted.

"No, not at all," I replied as calmly as I could. "You're the one sticking an Uzi in my face, so I don't think you're joking. Not one bit."

His eyes, outlined by holes in his ski mask, drilled into me and I stared back. There was silence.

"Through Satan's asshole," I whispered, eventually.

"Good," he spat back, "because I'm sure as fuck not making this up. This is Dante's idea—Dante's the one who went to hell, not me!"

And when I awoke, a fiery dragon stood before me.

    And he said, "Swallow the little scroll."

And he clutched the scroll in his outstretched claw.

    But I thought he had said "scrotum," and did nothing.

But when I closed my eyes, a fiery dragon awoke.

    His claw was a little scrotum, and everything became clear.

I swallowed the holy city, and nobody said a word:

    I was locked in Patty Hearst's closet.

      "Do you think I'm kidding or something, *motherfucker*?"

Birth

There was, once upon a time, a piece of wood. This wood was not valuable, it was only a common log like those burnt in winter in the stoves and fireplaces to make a cheerful blaze and warm the rooms. As the sharp axe stood suspended in the air above the wood, the old carpenter suddenly heard a small voice implore him, "Do not strike me so hard!" The carpenter turned his terrified eyes all around the room to try and discover where the little voice could possibly have come from, but he saw nobody.

Call me Isaac.

First born

First up

First cause

First smoke

First love

Genealogy

I was born in the year 1947, in the city of Brooklyn, of a good family, though not of that country, my father being a foreigner, of Lublin, who settled first in the Lower East Side. He got a good estate by merchandise, and extending his trade to textiles, lived afterwards in Queens, whence he had married my mother, whose relations were named Pesach, a very good family in Warsaw, and from whom I was called Pesach Hirsh. By the usual corruption of words on Ellis Island, we are now called, nay, we call ourselves, and write our name, Patty Hearst, and so my companions always called me.

Pinocchio's terrified eyes turn all around the room, but he sees nobody.
    And he cries out, "You are my father, and I am your son!"
But the father prefers to hum while he carves up the bone.
    By the usual corruption of words he is seen by nobody.

Mystery

The bare bulb hung directly above the upturned hood of the white Porsche. Through the open garage doors the dim sepia light reached into the night, illuminating the body of a man dressed in oil-splotched loafers, greasy wool Pendleton shirt, and dirty Levi's. He seemed to have been slumbering, napping beside his tool chest, except that his skull was savagely crushed in and his unblinking eyes stared out at a line of blood trickling down his cheek. It was Patty Hearst, the socialite playboy. Never again would he change the sparkplugs scattered on the floor.

"Do not strike me so hard," the boy implores him.

"Do you think I'm kidding or something, motherfucker?" he replies.
But "the usual" corrupts the words, and nothing is learned.

"Whichever way I write my name, the axe will hum."

Whichever way I write my name the axe will hum.

These songs claim descent from King David himself.
Yet the tunes of the well-to-do hardly fill the crushed skull's dome.

"Do you think I'm kidding or something, *motherfucker*?"

First come first served

Last hired first fired

First Things First

Whoever comes through the door first dies first

First Principles

Last Rites

Never again would he change the sparkplugs scattered on the floor.

But where else could the little voice possibly have come from?
He cannot dream except in words, and they are savagely crushed.

The sparkplugs speak by bridging gaps: "I am King David's Whore."

Christine's Dad

Bob is both cousin and brother to Christine since Alfredo is father to them both, although Christine's mom is Esther who is the sister of Edith, the mother of Bob. After he got back from Nam, Alfredo managed to get Edith pregnant before running off to San Francisco with Esther to father Christine. In order to run off with Alfredo, Esther had to flee Maurice, the father of her two boys she delivered against her will at the age of sixteen and seventeen. Maurice was so jealous he would not allow her to go to college, and he ate the same fish night after night (they had gone fishing and the freezer was stuffed with perch) until she felt she would have to starve or go crazy, so Esther had no choice but to take off. However, after awhile Alfredo ran off with his true love, cocaine, only to father one more son, Tommy, with Marianne, Esther's friend who had helped Esther track down Alfredo after he had kidnapped Christine. But Marianne had ended up falling into Alfredo's arms just the same, as did so many women, though Esther, with her new husband Howard and her friends and a private eye, did manage to corner Alfredo, and even though he waved a pistol in one hand with Christine—who was only five or six at the time—under his other arm, Esther and Howard were able to wrest the child away. Then Alfredo brought Esther to court to gain sole custody of Christine, accusing Esther of being an unfit mother because she was a terrorist who sold all of Christine's toys to raise money for the New People's Army back in the Philippines, but the suit was dropped immediately after Alfredo appeared on a TV documentary boasting that his cocaine habit was up to $700 a day—and it so happened that Christine was switching the channels when there appeared her father making his boast, although she had no idea what he was really saying, and she just stared at her father's face on the screen in silent wonder.

In any case, Alfredo had told Christine, now twenty-three, that he would die of cancer in six months—Agent Orange and all that. But a year had passed, and he was still very much alive.

"Aren't you supposed to be dead already?" Christine finally demanded.

This, then, is where our story begins, with the failure of Alfredo, Christine's father, to die.

Through the usual corruption of words
the bombardier can see
the bare breasts of Patty Hearst.

What kind of a game is that?

Delete.

Foreplay first
First she conquered, then he came
First Communion
Second Coming

This, then, is where our story begins,
with an axe about to carve out a boy,
the blood trickling down the carpenter's cheek.

All we have to do is crawl through Satan's asshole.

At last

History

I sit down to write somewhat concerning the life and character of Patty Hearst, a woman as remarkable in the annals of crime as any of the renowned robbers of the Old or New World who have preceded her. I do this, not for the purpose of ministering to any depraved taste for the dark and horrible in human action, but rather to contribute my mite to those materials out of which the history of California shall one day be composed.

First 0 songs for a prelude

Detective

It was the kind of frigid, late-night rain that reminds cats to come inside and curl up in front of a leaky space heater. That night the cats were not the only sensible creatures, since the dark street was empty except for stray SUVs lumbering through the intersection like sleek chrome dragons. If anyone in those bloated vehicles noticed me, they would have surely remarked that whoever battled these elements must have been a man pursued by demons—or a damn fool. And they were right. I was both.

First among equals

The First National Bank

The Party of the First Part

The first White Man to see the Grand Cherokee

First Church of Christ, Scientist

"Do not strike me so hard," the Bad Boy implored him.

He closed his eyes, but all he could see was the Grand Cherokee.

Smoke puffed from his nostril like a tiny exhaust, and he thought:

"If there is any example of the vernacular, it is Ford's Model-T."

The spring's first dandelion shows its trustful face.

Star light

Star bright

First star I see tonight

Part The First

Nobody said a word

Bad Boy

"How do you and your Pa get along now?" asked the grocery man of Pinocchio, as he leaned against the counter instead of sitting down on a stool, while Pinocchio bought a bottle of steroids.

"O, I don't know. He don't seem to appreciate me. What he ought to have is a deaf and dumb boy with only one leg and both arms broke—then he could enjoy a quiet life. But I am too rambunctious for Pa, and you needn't be surprised if you never see me again. I talk of running away with a circus, which is why I need the steroids. Since I played The Switch on Pa, there seems to have been a coldness in the family, and I sleep on the roof."

"The Switch," asked the store keeper, "what kind of a game is that?"

First impression
First prize
First Lady
First World

Orders

I went along with the order because, frankly, I did not think I would be allowed to carry out the command. I took the boy—innocently skipping along with his dad, unaware of the cruel edict—and went up to the top of Twin Peaks. All San Francisco glittered beneath us, and we marveled at the shimmering strange streak of Market Street as it cut diagonally across the right angles of the city's other streets. When I pulled out the butcher knife I closed my eyes and expected that the voice would say, "Enough! You have displayed enough of your foolish loyalty!" My eyes opened, but I could see nothing. I could hear nothing. I waited again, and I would not have done it, I would not have even thought of doing it, except that I had fully expected that my hand would be stayed and I would be told to butcher a stray dog instead. But I was led to believe that I was merely being tested, and in such manner I was betrayed.

"The countermand will come," I assured myself. "I must go ahead, allow myself to be fooled without appearing to know I am being toyed with, and by going ahead I will bring it to a halt."

In such fashion, I was condemned to obey.

Now there is a coldness in the family, and he sleeps on the roof.
Some orders are changed, but only to make sure that the rest never do.
Patty Hearst is the killer, although there is no proof.
According to Blockbuster, all God's movies are overdue.

"Well, there's always next time."

"This *is* the next time," mumbled the bombardier.

TWO

Home

After seventeen years of exile the political situation after the Oslo Agreement finally allowed my father to return home to Jerusalem from Chicago. When he arrived at the airport in Tel Aviv, his family and friends from the village crowded all around him. In a caravan of Mercedes *services* and other cars they drove back to the cluster of one-story stone houses on what they call French Hill. Out the window of the house he could see across the street to the playground and apartment building filled with Jews. The playground was for the Jewish kids, while the Palestinian children stayed away and played in the dusty street in front of the cluster of low stone houses. They always kept apart. Even though the Jews on French Hill were not the very violent settlers, it was still best to keep apart.

The apartment building had not even been built when my father had to flee the Israelis because of his militant activities in the first years of resistance to the occupation. But even so, he looked out the window at the land of his birth with deep satisfaction. Neighbors and old school chums came over, and there was great joy to see how the puny kid had become so brawny. My father worked for years in a metal stamping plant, lifting and hauling and shoving I-beams and other heavy chunks of steel, and he had become a man of great physical as well as moral strength.

Finally, after sitting in the cramped living room talking until late into the night with his mother and his brothers he had not seen in seventeen years, my father went to sleep in the very same bed of his youth. How delicious it all must have felt, I could only imagine. But in the darkness before dawn my father became restless, and he got up from his old bed and stared out that window at the blackness of the sky. He marveled to be home, even though he felt a cramp tightening in his arm. My grandmother arose along with her son, asking if there was anything wrong. My father only smiled wryly and said that all he needed was a cup of tea to make the cramp go away. Grandmother put the water on the stove, and my father went again to the window to look out at the first light of dawn spreading across the land he had known so long only in memory.

He looked out the window for a moment, quietly peering into the dim gray of dawn. Then his gentle smile turned to a grimace, he clutched his arm and fell to the floor with a thud that waked the entire house. In moments his family had gathered around him, calling for an ambulance, attempting to revive him, but to no avail. My father died in an instant, overcome by a massive heart attack.

The joyous celebration turned to a somber funeral, a memorial even stranger than all the other anguished angry funerals of the first *Intifada*. My father must have had the heart condition for some time without knowing it, but he had somehow, perhaps intuitively, managed to stay alive long enough to return home, long enough to drive through the roadblocks of the political situation's impossibilities, to complete the circle of his life's journey before his heart gave out. In the shock of his sudden collapse there was at least the bittersweet realization that his will had been so strong that he was able to come home, even if only to look out the window of his family's house one last time, before he died, a martyr to the persistence of memory.

One by one the friends and relatives found themselves by the window where he had stood. Without saying anything or drawing attention to themselves, they each paused a moment to look out at the view of the land that he had seen before the darkness closed over him. It was nothing picturesque or spectacular, simply a dull field of rocks sloping away, but one by one they peered through the window's frame, and it was as if they were viewing, for the very first time, a scene so sublime that the landscape took their breaths away.

At first glance

This is the first resurrection

The one and only

Second to none

One time only

None

No seconds allowed

INVALID

Murder

I woke up in the lab in the hills above Palo Alto, bleary-eyed, teeth chattering from the unusual cold. I had worked all night while nipping at my bottle of single malt Scotch until I had passed out. Now I stared through the window, peered out across to the East Bay, astonished that snow had actually fallen overnight, hardly a regular occurrence in the mild Bay Area. A haiku came to mind in an instant, despite my hangover. I almost never write poetry, especially something so alien and tortured as a haiku, but I quickly scratched it out on a message pad without any idea of what it meant:

Yolanda Ochoa in Robinson Mays

It was a man's deep gruff voice, and he was enraged. "Two customers fighting again," the cashier behind the counter at Robinson Mays winked knowingly. But when the voice grew louder, moving towards us, another sales-clerk said she was going to call security.

He was a cholo, mid-twenties, very tall, muscular, real buff, his head completely shaved, his pants excessively baggy, his checkered shirt loose, tattoos blazoned on his arms, and in those bulging arms he held a little boy no more than two or three years old. The baby was bawling as his father screamed, "You fucking asshole! Don't you ever fucking do this to me again, do you understand?" As he slapped the little boy in his face and legs, grabbing him by the collar, screaming into his face, a young woman fol-lowed behind, her hair disheveled, bleached blonde, her clothes shabby, her face blotched from tears as she cowered behind her husband like a scared dog following her master.

The whole crowd stood paralyzed, staring at the man. "What the hell are you looking at? *Mind your own fucking business*," he hollered at them. Still, everyone stood trans-fixed, unable to move. I glanced at my sister and I knew she was thinking of her own son, and when she paced quickly after the cholo I hissed out to her, "*Esperanza! What are you doing? You don't want to mess with these people!*"

She didn't hear a word I said, and when she went up to the man I felt a sudden pang of fear. I ran to where she was, stopping abruptly to hear what she was telling him.

"Hey, mister, please calm down. I don't want to get into your business or anything, but what you're doing is wrong. Look at the boy, since maybe you don't know you're hurting him. I have a son his age too, and I know that you're getting nowhere by treating him like this. He's just a little boy."

Maybe because my sister spoke calmly and the cholo could see the anguish in her eyes, or maybe because the fury that had overtaken him had been spent, he answered her quietly and without menace. "He is my son and I love him. It's just that he doesn't listen. I was so scared. He ran off and I couldn't find him. I thought I had lost him."

"Do you think he understands what he did wrong?" my sister continued. "He is so frightened, and he's just a little boy. He's just curious, like my own little boy. At this age they just want to roam around and see everything. It's not their fault. They're just little boys."

Then the man started to cry, saying he loved his son so very much. He turned to his boy, who was still screaming, and said, "Sorry, *mijo*, we are going to buy you a motorcycle right now." All throughout, the bleached-blonde mom stood alongside, weeping. "You know, I don't doubt you love your son," my sister told the *cholo*. "My father loves us, always has, but like you he doesn't know how to deal with his love and control his anger. I can tell you from personal experience that you are not gaining your child's love, only his fear."

Then the police arrived on the scene and all hell broke loose.

Dawn's light–

Booze all night–

   "Truth Table Detects Valid Code:

   No God—Just Snow!"

Ceremony

Under certain circumstances there are few hours in life more agreeable than the hour dedicated to the ceremony known as "rolling a joint." There are circumstances in which, whether you partake of the herb or not—some people of course never do—the situation is in itself delightful. Those that I have in mind in beginning to unfold this simple history offered an admirable setting to an innocent pastime.

NOTICE

Persons who have been prosecuted will find a motive in this narrative; persons who have been banished will find a moral in it; persons who have been shot will find a plot in it.

**BY ORDER OF THE AUTHOR
PER D. D., CHIEF OF ORDURE**

The first step in designing an Invalid Code Detector is to develop the Truth Table.

The Truth Table shows all possible input states and their resulting outputs.

The Gate makes its decision according to the input state and its particular function.

The Gate generates the appropriate binary output, either one or zero, which is then recorded as the Truth.

If one input is zero then all outputs will be zero, no matter the signal on the other input, according to the Law of Intersection.

Yet, O Law of Union, you appear almost perverse: no matter the input signal the same output signal will result.

But when the same signal is applied to all inputs, two ones or two zeros, the identical output will result, either one or zero, as inscribed by the Law of Tautology.

To unfold this simple history, partake of the snow, and then record the results.

Murder

When I woke up in the lab and saw the woman's body sprawled across the laptop I knew she was dead. I didn't recognize her and had no idea how she got inside the lab. I had no clue how she had died; I had no idea how moist blood came to be smeared across my torn shirt, nor how my pants came to be pulled down to my ankles.

None of this looked good.

I ran to the window to barf.

One Big Union

One Happy Family

One Way

One God

One never knows, do one?

Instructions for Reading

A sketchy affair. Sly humor peeps out occasionally, though buried under quite too many words, and you read on and on, expecting something more than you ever find, to be choked off at the end of the book like the audience of a Turkish story teller, without getting the end of the story.

To unfold this simple history, expect something more than you ever find.

"Do you think he understands what he did wrong?"

He marvels to be home, though it is buried under quite too many words.

Only the end of the story is holy, according to the Laws of Tautology.

How do I love thee? Let me count the ways:

ONE

One day my prince will come

One-up-man-ship

One day at a time

Bedtime Story

"Will we ever get to the end of the story?"

"I'm afraid not, darling. If we come to the end of the story we will die, the king will kill us, and we want to avoid that, don't we?"

"So death is the end of the story, Mother?"

"No, my little princess, it's the other way around: the end of the story means death, and that's why we keep the story going night after night after night."

"But what if we never begin?"

"Don't start up with me again!"

Mark Twain's Idea

Artemus Ward really wanted to be a comic actor and not a humorous lecturer. In Virginia City he got drunk, slipped away, smeared burnt cork on his face and joined a minstrel troupe, playing goofy end man to the pompous interlocutor. But he was soon recognized by someone in the audience despite his blackface, and in response to howls of delight and insistent demands, he was forced to give up the minstrel act and embark upon one of his rambling, disconnected, incoherent, mumbling lectures. The crowd thought his performance funnier than ever, perhaps because the blackface heightened his lugubrious incongruity even more.

Finally, he left the stage, feeling humiliated despite the roars of the audience, and he blamed Mark Twain for the whole debacle. "Why didn't you stop me from making a fool of myself?" he demanded of the Nevada journalist who stood in the wings.

But Twain just gave him a quizzical look as he pondered the situation. "What would it be like to give such a bizarre lecture," he mused to himself, "but to deliver it while wearing *invisible* blackface?"

ONE NATION UNDER GOD
One move and I'll blow your head off!
One out
One of these days, Pow! Right in the kisser!

Masturbation Journal

Why I decided to keep a masturbation journal I am not sure. Certainly the IRS does not need the record to verify tax write-offs. I wanted to keep an account of the nature of my fantasies rather than to keep any notation of time or frequency. How will I know ten years from now what provided a likely excuse to jack off? What yanked the pleasure from my loins other than my hand? Perhaps twenty or thirty years from now, old and shriveled, I will not even be able to remember the overwhelming urge to whip out my dick and pump it to life. If such were the case, I could return to my journal and refresh stale memory with notes of its old arousals, and by the presence in my hand of the journal's bulk I could then recall the heft of my dick in my hand years before. Is this art? The shift from dick to page and back again? Well, that is too much to consider for me; just so long as I can still tug the root of all desire with little or no reflection, I have no need for art.

Prophetic Attractions

When she began to write reviews of movies before they were released she was just an unremarkable white girl, a freshman at Queens College. Whether she considered a film good or bad was something to note, but what was truly uncanny was how she had a full knowledge of the film even before it had been screened publicly. Scenes, dialogue, shots, special effects, all of it. Had she seen a pirated video? Had she gotten secret access to screening rooms? She explained that she had no inside peek, but that she could see the film quite simply roll before her eyes. Sometimes when waiting for a subway, or other times when watching something altogether different on TV, or even when walking through Flushing Meadows Park, she would be able to see an unreleased movie in place of greenery or MTV or the F train, and at the end she would write down her description of it and her opinion and send it off to *Newsday* or some other newspaper. It was as simple as that.

At first the newspapers ignored her reviews. But when *Independence Day* was released, one of the editors at Newsday was sure that he had read the president's stirring Fourth of July speech moments before the motley force of pilots took off to save the earth from alien invaders long in advance of the movie's first press release. The memory gnawed at him, until he realized it had come from one of the girl's letters. He got in contact with her, and she began to write reviews of other movies before they were released, which were printed in the movie section under the heading "Prophetic Attractions."

After reviews of *There's Something about Mary* (she liked it) and other films appeared six months before the movies were released, she became a sensation. She was treated as a curiosity by many, while Hollywood regarded her as something vaguely threatening. Others claimed her as someone with a supernatural gift who was blessed with a special mission, like one of those little girls who can spot the Blessed Virgin Mary's face in a gum wrapper. The more secular considered her possessed of a keen imagination and a unique intuition concerning the Hollywood mind. Others, especially film distributors and owners of movie houses, became increasingly uneasy about the thumbsup or thumbsdown ratings she gave to these yet-to-be-released flicks.

But when she began to write reviews of movies even before they were produced, the uproar was deafening. Scripts under development locked up in safes or options filed away in drawers or even scribbled ideas circulating around studios suddenly became full-blown cinematic creations. She could see what was just a nub of an idea as a completely rendered film, actors and all, even before the stars had signed a contract, and she would write down the film's plot, critique the acting, and tender her thumbs up or thumbs down somewhat placidly, as if there were nothing at all odd about reviewing films that had not yet even come into existence. Hollywood executives became hysterical. Law suits were in the air, rumors of bribes to pay her off or threats by nervous gangsters began to circulate.

Then CIA agents in black suits approached her about preserving her gift for national security purposes. They were polite but insistent, as they sat in her parents' living room. And she listened to them, somewhat baffled as they spoke to her of "intelligence" they had received that an Islamic terrorist group or the Russian Mafia was planning to kidnap her because they believed she could see weapons systems on the drawing boards even before they were built or stock market crashes long before the plunge. When the agents left, still polite, the girl and her parents doubted the terrorist story, but they were certain that the agents were themselves interested in employing her powers for more than entertainment purposes.

That's when she and her parents became genuinely alarmed. Something had to be done, they felt, or else she would be killed by gangsters or whisked off by anxious agents to some secret Area 51.

Murder

When I woke up in the lab and saw the man's body sprawled across the laptop I knew he was dead. I didn't recognize him and had no idea how he got inside the lab. I had no clue how he had died, and I had no idea how moist blood came to be smeared across my torn blouse, nor how my skirt came to be pulled over my head.

None of this looked good.

I ran to the window to barf.

Masturbation Journal

Butthole—pussy flaps wide open, rear end view —*Hustler*

3-way orgy scene—throbbing cock about to plunge —*Penthouse*

Precocious parochial school girl on Mission St.—plaid skirt, high socks, panty peeking out—unbearable—I run to my room and yank out dick

Taking a pee, I can see out bathroom window across alley to next-door gay neighbors who, legs askew on bed,

hump. I can only see feet and ankles, both turned in
the same direction, but can hear the groans: I join
them over the toilet, a secret fudge-packer threesome
"Maria"—Mexican girl with globular boobs, tight slit, lan-
guid smile —*Hustler*
Scrambled porno TV channel—video wiggly but audio
clear of woman's moans and groans and shrieks of
"Yes! Yes! Yes! *Fuck me!*" I fuck her

A Flip-Flop remembers, as perhaps nothing else can, its previous state.
To think logically requires both a capability for making decisions based
on given information and the ability to remember them.
Logic circuits accept input binary data, and with their built-in decision
making capability, they generate the appropriate output binary
signals.
Flip-Flops store Truth for later use, and when arranged in cascades of
sequential circuits they can shift, manipulate, and otherwise make
ghosts appear before our very eyes.

Masturbation Journal

"Maria"—dark eyes—tight slit
Victoria's Secret
Woke up with hard-on, kept it hard all morning at work
rubbing between my legs, gave it what it wanted in
bathroom during coffee break, no fantasy required
"Maria"—pouting lips—pouting slit
Phone Sex Ads: "Pump My Rump"—"I'm Barely Legal"—
"Cum-Lovin' Slut"

Call up "Pump My Rump"—photo of bare butthole, cunt
    flaps open from rear, black leather boots up to thigh—I
    pump her rump as instructed
Soft sheets in the morning
Clear blue sky

Job Experience

Rachel got fired for being too sad.

"There's no reason to use a frying pan," Rachel had
thought in a flash as she saw the black, greasy metal come
down on her head. "I'd give you the keys to my car, money,
everything. Just ask. No need to smash my skull." An
instant later she couldn't think at all, and the three kids
who she had counseled at the halfway house for delinquent
teenagers—she had naively thought they were her
friends—ran off while she took a terrible nap, clobbered
and bloody, on the floor.

The very next day the dumb kids were caught, but it
took weeks for the dozens of stitches to heal and months
for her to get over the not-so-strange feelings that she
couldn't trust anyone, especially teenagers. She wasn't
much older than a teenager herself, and she had wanted to
be a pediatric psychologist, which is why she had taken the
job at the halfway house in the first place, a way to get
experience, although getting beaten nearly to the point of
death was not the experience she had had in mind. Now
she wasn't so sure what her career path would be, and she
had to spend more months with counselors just to get past
the trauma, to dissolve the queasy aftertaste of terror.

That's why working at the pottery store—one of those
places where people come in and pick their undecorated

plate or bowl or pitcher, paint it up, then put it in the kiln themselves—seemed such an ideal place. Customers came in, browsed, doodled over a pot, zigzags and lizards and other designs flowing onto the surfaces from their inner-most souls, and she would doodle with them, they would smile, she would slip the clay into the kiln, and the next day she could see the delight of satisfied customers picking out their treasures.

Her boss would coo and smile effusively at her like a somewhat irritating, overdone party hostess. Rachel would nod back, smiling weakly, and resume dabbing and painting and doodling with the customers.

None of this prepared her for getting fired for being "too sad."

"Your disability is affecting your work," the Luella Parsons of the pottery wheel declared.

Rachel knew that wasn't true. Customers enjoyed her subdued, business-like, yet pleasing demeanor. They were the ones having fun, not her, the lizards crawling from their brains, not hers, and she would make the customers feel that their playing around with pottery was just serious enough not to be ridiculous or utterly childish.

"I suppose I didn't gush back enough at my boss," she thought, "but why should I? Her toothy smile turned out to be just another kind of frying pan."

One for the Road

HILTON OBENZINGER

Prophetic Attractions

"Come in," cried the editor.

The door of the editorial room of PARANORMAL SEX began to creak painfully under the hesitating presence of an uncertain and unfamiliar hand. This continued until, with a start of irritation, the editor faced directly about, throwing his leg over the arm of his chair with a certain youthful dexterity. With one hand gripping its back, the other still grasping a photo proof sheet, and his pencil in his mouth, he stared at the intruder, a young brunette in a short blue skirt and a simple white oxford blouse.

"Do you know who I am?"

The editor swiveled fully around in his chair to give the pretty college girl the once-over.

"No, I don't," he confessed, pulling the pencil from out of his mouth. "How can I help you?"

"I thought this was the editorial office for PARA-NORMAL SEX?"

"It is, and I am the editor. But I'm not a psychic, if that's what you mean. In fact, the publishers were pretty adamant that what they wanted was a professional to run a magazine and not a mind reader. So, what can I do for you, Miss—?"

She simply told him her name.

"Oh, yes," the editor recognized the name immediately. "You're that girl who writes movie reviews before the films are released. 'Prophetic Attractions' in *Newsday*, right? Very astonishing, a real gift. And now I hear that you're doing reviews of movies even before they've been shot, even before they've been hatched from the producer's noggin. How can you do that?"

She smiled. "I don't know how I do any of it, but I do know that you can save my life."

"Me? Save your life? Don't kid around."

She wasn't kidding. She went on with a bizarre story of how Hollywood, irritated over her meddling in their plans, may have put a contract out on her. But worse yet, there were even darker forces—maybe the CIA, maybe terrorists—who thought her powers could be put to other, more sinister uses.

"That's why I've come to you."

He could only offer a puzzled look.

"I want to pose nude, an entire spread, even a centerfold, in *PARANORMAL SEX*."

His perplexed look changed to pure astonishment. *"You want to do what?"*

"I know this sounds crazy, but just listen for a moment. If I pose nude in your magazine, and thousands of men see me, and they fantasize about having sex with me, play with themselves, or whatever, I am sure, I am absolutely certain, this will somehow drain off the power I have been cursed with. Each erection, each fantasy, each private ejaculation—well, it's like some kind of equation. Somehow I know this—don't ask me how. I only know that when I expose my breasts and spread my legs, when these men drool over my naked body, my clairvoyant powers will dissolve with each throb of their . . ." and she blushed. "I know if I do this I will be set free," she continued, "and Hollywood gangsters or the CIA or God himself will have no need to bother themselves with me again."

The editor stroked his chin and made a fresh appraisal of the girl.

He noted that she was cute enough, that was certain, though she was not all that buxom. Still, the publicity, the notoriety, the inevitable astronomical leap in circulation made up for any shortcomings in her equipment, and he could even arrange for implants, if need be. His mouth suddenly went dry, and he licked his lips. But his calculations of skyrocketing ad revenues and fantasies of raucous press conferences were cut short when she began to unbutton her blouse.

"Not yet," he said as he stopped her hand, a sly grin creeping over his face.

BEGIN HERE
START NOW

Adventures of Injun Joe

You don't know about me without you have read a book by the name of *The Adventures of Tom Sawyer*, but that ain't no matter. That book was made by Mr. Mark Twain, and he told lies, mainly. There was things which he said that was true or half true, but mainly he stretched a pack of lies and made it all come out his way. For instance, the book winds up with Tom and Huck finding the money that I and my partners hid in the cave, and it made them rich. That was true enough, spitefully so, but he also said they found me scratching at the door of the cave, dead and moldy, and as you can see that ain't so. It was one of my partners who died, and when I spotted the little pinhole of light that meant a branch of the cave would lead me to freedom, I switched clothes with him so people would think that old moldy body was Injun Joe who had up and gone to hell when in fact I was making my way across the river, up north, across Illinois, traveling all the way to New York City where I got me another, even bigger treasure speculatin' on Wall Street. Now I'm all weighed down with gold, far more than the six thousand dollars Tom and Huck each got. No, I ain't dead, unless being powerful rich means I'm dead and gone to my just reward. And I aim to return to St. Petersburg, I do. Well, not exactly in the flesh, since they might still be fixing to hang me, but I do have enough cash to have my lawyers buy every house, every store, every stitch of land, every soul in the entire, miserable, low-down, mean-spirited town. Any other man would have been satisfied to murder two or three of 'em and call it even, but to me that would have been a petty revenge, and inadequate, for the dead do not *suffer*.

Each holy city was like some kind of equation.
When I opened my eyes, all I could see were films that were not yet made.
Then my Flip-Flop returned, and I remembered a private ejaculation.
"Do you think I'm kidding or something, *motherfucker*?" God said.

Last Words

After they pulled the gurney out of the room they left his mother to wait in the hallway before rolling her into the operating room. A triple bypass has become almost commonplace nowadays, but you still take your life in your hands any time you go under the knife, especially if you're in your seventies.

His mother had been nervous and frightened beforehand, but now she was calm, even casual, probably a result of sedatives.

"I'll be alright," she said, taking his hand as she looked up from the gurney. Then he was startled by her laugh.

"Ha! Ha! I just remembered something. Why remember this I don't know, and why now. Soon after I came to America, and I was still a greenhorn, though I had already met your father, I was sitting on the stoop of our apartment house in Brooklyn when a man came up to me, a neat, well-dressed man, and he said, 'Do you want me to give you a blow job?'"

She laughed some more, and her son, trying to be nonchalant, felt compelled to correct his mother: "You know, you probably remember it wrong. Most likely he was asking if you would give HIM a blow job, given how the expression is usually employed."

"But I think he said it that way. My English was not yet good, so I went running up the stairs, four flights, to ask your father.

"'Who said this to you?' he demanded, and he was ready to run downstairs and punch the man in the face."

Then she giggled, and grew quiet.

"Here I am," she sighed, "right before getting cut open, and I remember this? Of all things, the man sixty years ago who asked me do I want a blow job? I could die under the knife and this could be my last words?"

The nurses arrived to wheel her away, and she waved one final time, laughing goodbye, before she disappeared through the shiny metallic doors.

THREE

Gary Gone Postal

Gary was the last person we expected to see when we answered the doorbell, but there he was, climbing up the stairs, talking a mile a minute about gangs in San Diego and how he had barely escaped their clutches by fleeing to Elko, Nevada, although now his enemies had discovered his whereabouts, so he needed to get away, lay low, which is why the bus driver—who he insisted was a member of his own gang, a true friend—brought him to San Francisco, right to our doorstep.

"Hey, gook! Your mother's a whore who fucks gooks!"

Displayed on Gary's forehead and left cheek was an intricate cobweb of scars.

Gary had, quite literally, Gone Postal.

Gary's troubles really all began with the car accident, that time when Gary and his cousins all piled into the vastness of the borrowed Chrysler after Evelyn's wedding party, and Chris lost control at the exit to downtown Monterey, the thick luxury car smashing into an even thicker tree.

Although Gary thought of himself as a handsome, suave operator, when his face was cut and scarred as the result of a car accident, the main thing that he thought he had going for him, his looks, was violently, irrevocably torn away.

"I used to deliver up and down Malibu, driving up to the mailboxes and popping in letters to the stars," Gary would boast, "and I'd see what's-his-name, the short guy in *Taxi*,

Danny DeVito, and I'd tell him my latest jokes. He got half his material from me!"

Gary picked up a huge file cabinet in the sorting room and threw it at the fucker who insulted his mother.

When he grabbed a pair of scissors to lunge after the letter carrier who called his mother a whore, it took five big guys to pull him to the floor.

The union official felt badly that they hadn't filed charges against the long-term tormentor who had pushed Gary over the edge—after all, the racist jerk was the true instigator—but at least they worked it out so the Post Office would give Gary his job back, if only he would make a few visits to a shrink.

"Crank can do that to you, can rip out your brains, and you end up wandering night after night with no sleep, no food," Eddie informed us, sagely. "And the speed replaces those brains with old slasher movies turned inside out, pure paranoid death, until wherever Gary may be— whether he's in a minimart donut shop or he's on a bus or he's in your living room—wherever he is, that place becomes the new location for *Psycho*'s Bates Motel."

```
Dear Aunt and Uncle,
Greetings from your nephew Gary.
Remember me? HA HA! I've missed your
responses in the past. The reason I'm
writing you both is I want you to buy
```

and <u>read</u> the <u>PRince of DARKness</u>
<u>ANtiCHRist AND THE NEW WORLD ORDER</u>

THE AUTHOR IS GRANT R. JEFFREY

LOVE GARY

P.S. ESPecially Read CHAPter 4.

"I'm getting some big moola from the car insurance for the accident," Gary winked at his bewildered aunt and uncle, "so I need to borrow your car to get to L.A."

> Sometimes you want to destroy momentarily
> the stability of perception
> and inflict a kind of voluptuous panic
> upon an otherwise lucid mind.

Return to the Klamath

"Here, the Spirit is still in everything—the trees, the rocks, the river," the Indian explained, pointing at the Klamath. "The concrete world of the white man is kind of dead, like something's missing and the people are afraid. That's why this place is just right for me."

In order for the Forest Service to complete the GO Road linking Gasquet and Orleans they would have to violate the peace of Doctor Rock.

"I was a building contractor and was doing alright—nice big homes around Modesto," Tiger said with a slightly embarrassed shrug, "then I decided to come home to the Klamath."

"Jews don't need a river, a single piece of land," I explained to Tiger, who stared at me with a troubled, perplexed look. "We carry our homes in our heads. It's like there's a Doctor Rock always in my skull."

I had been invited back to the Yurok Reservation twenty-five years after teaching at the two-classroom schoolhouse, to say a few words to the four kids graduating the eighth grade.

"*Aw, they're acting like a bunch of NIGGERS,*" Tiger, the oldest boy had shot back when I returned from Alcatraz with posters and stories of the occupation after Christmas break in 1969; but the thirteen-year-old kid in the seventh grade ended up growing into a wiry, handsome leader of his people.

Tiger had fought to stop the GO Road from cutting through areas sacred to the Yuroks, Karoks, and Hoopas, with such determination, had become such a pain in the ass and for such a long time, seventeen years—even though the Supreme Court had declared that "freedom of religion" did not protect those high places where the women who become Indian Doctors go to learn their calling—that Congress finally threw in the towel and stopped the road and declared Doctor Rock and the other mountain places to be an untouched "wilderness area."

I like to think that Tiger's becoming a pain in the ass had something to do with me.

Twenty-five years later, most of the men I had known who worked in the woods—Skunk, Frosty, Tiger's dad, others—were dead from cancer, and everyone knew that the sickness came from the herbicides the logging companies keep on spraying to cut back the bush.

"Why would I live anywhere else?" Tiger swept his arm to the Klamath glittering at the bottom of the steep, plummeting cliffs right outside his door, then to the hills and to the circling sky, a vista of vast, dizzying proportions.

When I called out to the classroom as part of a math problem, "TWO PLUS TWO EQUALS . . . ," Tiger—the oldest if not the biggest kid in the entire fifth-to-eighth grade classroom—hollered back, *"White man, you LIE!"*

So many of the boys I had taught twenty-five years ago are dead or in jail.

"You actually know things, things that other people don't know, you know about the river and all the rocks and creeks, everything about this place, the Klamath, and that's special, something no one else knows, and something no one else can take away from you," I concluded my few remarks at the graduation ceremony. Hank, the old school board member from the days I taught at the isolated school on the reservation, slid up behind me afterwards and whispered, "You talked too long," then slipped away. I spoke only two minutes or so, but I knew what he was really telling me: I had violated some sense of propriety; I had turned the spotlight away from the kids, filled up too much space, or some gaff like that. I smiled ruefully to myself. After twenty-five years, I end up failing the Yuroks one more time.

Every generation has its own wardrobe,
its own scenery,
its own mask.

Edwin in Queens

Why did the boy believe that his father was still alive in New York?

Edwin told the police that his family had all been killed in a mudslide during Hurricane Mitch and that he had traveled all the way from Honduras to find his father. Clutched in his hand, the boy had a letter from his father, with instructions to rendezvous with him at an overpass near La Guardia Airport.

In the end, what Edwin did was not a real crime that causes any harm; if anything, it was just a misdemeanor of the heart.

Edwin's father had actually died the year before of what they call complications from AIDS, yet the boy refused to believe it, and he had traveled to New York from his aunt's home in Hialeah with nothing more than the power of his delusion to find him.

All dead fathers come back to life in New York City. Everybody knows that.

"The press should have credited the story with 'the boy says, and the proper authorities have invested it with a great deal of credibility,' so we wouldn't look like we swallowed Edwin's story, hook, line, and sinker, but we didn't," the reporter confessed. "We wanted so much to believe the kid because it was one of those page-one stories of grit and determination that makes you think people can do anything, absolutely anything, when love and courage combine—the kind of story that every newspaperman dreams of, a poignant nugget of Truth that makes life worth living, even if it is a lie."

The story had appeared on the news for a day or two, and when it turned out to have been fabricated, the little boy of great heart that had astounded all of New York instantly disappeared from TV; Edwin, like his father, vanished without a trace.

God laughed seven times: *Ha-Ha-Ha-Ha-Ha-Ha-Ha.*
God laughed, and from these seven laughs
seven lesser gods sprang up which embrace the whole universe.
But when God laughed for the last time,
he drew in his breath, and while he was laughing he began to cry,
and thus the Soul came into being.

Father

In one week I learned that I am the father of three sons of three different mothers.

Well, perhaps I sired them, but I was no true father, at least not theirs. In fact, I had no idea that the brief encounters decades ago had produced anything more than vague memories, much less kids. But for some strange reason—and don't talk to me about coincidence—all three sons, each unaware of the other, decided to contact me at exactly the same time.

I remembered their mothers, sort of.

The oldest boy was the offspring of a date during college—she hung around with a crowd of girls that liked to fuck. In fact, each room of their apartment in Queens was filled with couples fucking, and we had to share her bedroom with another grunting pair. This was fun, but that was it.

The second boy's mother was a Jesus freak I had met in Santa Fe while visiting a friend who was hiding out there as a political fugitive from the FBI. The Jesus freak traveled with a crowd who frequented a beautiful, grand house occupied by a beautiful, grand woman—warm, delightful, friendly, statuesque, hospitable to all, sexy as hell—and she was the one I really wanted to sleep with. But she was the girlfriend of Gregory Corso or Neal Cassidy or somebody, so I had to settle for the pudgy though somewhat cute girl who seemed to adore me, and we made love in the hallway in a sleeping bag. She was very sweet, though I had no idea she was part of a Jesus freak commune outside Taos, and when I found out the next morning I ran like hell back to my friend's clandestine hideout.

The third son's mother was someone I met in Portland at a commune, notable because at least two of its members were wounded at the Kent State massacre, one of them with a shattered hand, and the other in a wheelchair for life, and everyone in the commune was very "heavy," preparing for armed struggle, taking their rifles every day out to the woods to shoot at targets. I crashed only a couple of nights, and she had no intention of contacting me again, seeing as how she was preparing to go underground, so it was a poignant, brief moment of crisscrossing lives in the Revolution. I often wondered what had happened to her.

Well, those were different times. I believed each one was on the pill and I never imagined we had conceived any children—and if we had, I would have expected to have heard from either or all of them much sooner. But each mother had decided she wanted to handle things on her own and chose not to seek me out, and only when their sons had grown older had the gnawing desire to find their biological father taken hold of them.

Now I held letters with photos declaring that I am the father of a recovering junky, a Pentecostal preacher, and an electrical engineer, and all three of them want to meet me—soon.

I am told the Pentecostal preacher, whose mother is the sex maniac, looks exactly like his father.

The Father is Child to the Man

Explanation

"See, what's great about America is that everyone can get a fresh start," the prisoner explained to the reporter. "You fuck up, sure, but you can take out a new lease on life and give it another whirl. That's all I'm asking, another chance, another day.

"Sure, I did wrong, though if you knew all the circumstances maybe you'd be a little bit sympathetic to my situation.

"It was like this: my father was sick, real sick, heart problems, and it didn't look good. He was old, his time was up, but all you can do is hope. I had to go all the way to Pennsylvania, and I wanted Helen to come with me, which is fitting for a wife, since this is a once in a lifetime event, the death of one's father, the only one I got. Am I right?

"But to my utter surprise Helen says no, says she can't get away from her job. Besides, her mother, who lives down the street, has her own health problems. I say, get someone else to take care of your mother and tell your job to shove it—priorities are priorities—but she gets stubborn.

"I never saw anything like it. A man's father is on his death bed, and his own wife can't see it in herself to do the right thing. It hurt, it hurt really bad. Can you imagine a thing like that?

"She only showed up in time for the funeral.

"Right then and there I plotted revenge, and I knew exactly how to do it so Helen would be tormented for the rest of her life.

"Helen always wanted a baby, been talking an earful for years, and I always put her off, figuring we got a hard enough time putting food on the table for the two of us.

"But now, with the death of my father, I suddenly change my mind. She's all gushy, and I oblige her, poking

HILTON OBENZINGER

her every chance I can to get her pregnant, and soon, sure enough, she balloons up like a toad's throat.

"Little Tyler is born, and she loves him up and coos and is overflowing with all the good things in life. But I wait for my chance. I figure Helen needs to get real attached to the little brat, let her get to cuddle and do all the baby things women love, and then I'll make my move.

"Three months or so after the kid is born I'm watching him take a nap when Helen is out. This was my chance, so I shove a pillow over his head and smother him. . . . "

The reporter noted the matter-of-fact way he recounted the murder, pausing to light a Marlboro, and then continued.

"It really wasn't too hard."

He took a long puff.

"Helen felt bad when she thought the kid died from the sudden death syndrome, and I chuckled to myself. Finally, I told her, 'Now you know how I felt when you wouldn't come with me to my dad when he was dying.'

"But now I know in the end it was a mistake. I lost everything. I lost my house, my job, my freedom, my wife, all my money, my car, everything."

"What about killing the kid?" the reporter asked.

"Yeah, I even lost the kid," he nodded.

"But all I'm asking for is another chance, a new start. This is America, so I figure I got the right to try again. Am I right?"

Sex is a monstrous delusion, a sleight-of-hand,

that equates authentic, though scientifically inaccurate,

Experience

with Truth.

Child

In the blinding light I could see Mary Magdalene with an infant. And Mary said, "This is Jesus, the child you have conceived, and I am his mother."

But how could I be the father of the Divine Child?

And she answered my unspoken question, "Because the child is within you, and you have resurrected the flesh through the purity of your soul, for you too are the Father."

I very much doubted the purity of my soul, but the Child looked at me and said, "I am the Legos." And he began to build an entire world with the small colored interlocking plastic blocks all spread out before him.

"I will build you a home," he said with a mischievous grin, and he molded mud into little people and when he blew on them they came to life and populated the small city he was constructing. Toying with a red block, he continued with the same sly grin, "I will build you a home, and when I am done, you will pay me the rent."

But then he grew weary, and in one swift blow he swept the small city away with the back of his hand. All of the city's inhabitants were killed in an instant, and he just looked up at me with innocent eyes, smiling, completely unaware of the havoc he had caused.

We live within the confines of money,
framed by concrete abstractions of time and space,
the vigor and turbulence of the circulation of capital,
all always under the ambiguous surveillance of the State.

HILTON OBENZINGER

Yearbook

My parents were finally too old to remain "snowbirds," flying to Florida for the winter and returning each spring, and I had come to help them move out of their house on Long Island to relocate permanently to those tropical climes. It was when I cleared away the stack of old magazines and papers on the wicker table in their den that I pulled from the bottom of the pile a copy of my junior–high school yearbook. I hadn't seen the yearbook for nearly forty years, and they lived in that house for almost thirty, which meant that they moved the yearbook from one house to another, placing it on the coffee table and leaving it there as they watched TV through the seventies, eighties, nineties. I had even forgotten that I had *had* a junior–high school yearbook, but there it was: photos of forgotten schoolmates, a little sappy poem I had written, "best wishes" and autographs and goofy remarks scribbled on its pages.

It was remarkable that the little piece of memorabilia had remained in the same spot for so many years, while all the times I had visited my parents it was there before my very eyes without my even knowing it. Even more remarkable is that I remembered only a few of the faces and names in the photos. I was surprised to learn that I had worked on the yearbook, yet even with the evidence of my standing for a group photo with the staff, I could not recall it. Here was proof of my past, photos of a young kid, yet I was looking at a virtual stranger, a phantom from a different era.

Then I turned the page, and there was the picture of the most beautiful girl in the whole world.

Concepts arise from collision,
the violent impossibility
giving form to new life.

Instructions for Living

Consider all of life as a visit to the Grand Canyon or Eiffel Tower. Do you really see the canyon? Do you truly ponder the tower? No, what you encounter is a series of postcards, of snapshots, of checklists to which you apply your latest mark: "Ah, yes, Grand Canyon: *Check!*" Everything is surrounded by the appurtenances of its remembrance, so you live in contact not with the thing itself but with its representation, its image, its what-every-one-says-it-is as accumulated over years, decades, centuries, and you have no desire to do otherwise. In fact, you can't, and your whole goal in life is to collect as many sights as you can, along with their postcards, ashtrays, pennants, thimbles, without end. You have no home, really, to which you can return once you have greased the wheels of semiotics. No, you simply return each night to what seems a long-term hotel room, a way station on your travels that you happen to carry on your back. All of life is beaten paths and the occasional adventure "off the beaten path," even your lovers or your children. Oh, how you squeal with delight at your adventures, not realizing that even your escapes are accounted for simply because you are part of a larger game, a tour package that embraces all of existence. No longer authentic, the world seems flimsy, and after a time you cannot even determine if anything could have ever been authentic in the first place, while the notion of "the first place" itself seems ridiculous. The native customs at the shopping mall seem as bizarre as ever, yet you have a dreary sense that the teenage mating rituals and the elaborate performances of "consumer confidence" are merely staged for your benefit, and while you are pleased that you are the audience, you are also depressed by the fact that you can never leave the show. No, you are the Eternal Tourist, and you will be buried in the Tomb of the Unknown Tourist. Crowds will gather at the Tomb—yet one more tourist sight—and they will weep because the bronze plaque tells them to remember that you were once like them.

How can foresight be an act of knowledge?

Detective

I felt it was strange when Patty Hearst phoned my office that warm spring day, and I could visualize her angular face, her thin, sharp nose as she spoke. But her life had been scrutinized endlessly—she had even written her own account of her strange interlude with the SLA—so why in the world did she need a detective, an archaeologist of the living, to rummage around in her life's lost-and-found?

"Tania," she half-whispered into the phone. "*I'm looking for Tania.*"

Parent-Teacher Conference

"I had no idea anything was wrong, but for six months my son was climbing out his bedroom window and wandering the streets at night because voices told him to. Finally, he confided in me that the voices started telling him to cut off his testicles, so that's when I knew he had to go to a hospital."

The high-school physics teacher divulged her story rapidly, excitedly. Months of hospital, a year or so of medication, and the realization made by herself and her son that he was "just wired differently than other people," and the voices were gone, at least for now.

All I had asked for was a way for my son to make up work from his physics class after his stay in the mental hospital. I had not expected this torrent of anguish. She would make sure my son would pass, but her understanding had to come with a price, the sharing of her own encounter with psychotic delusion.

I discovered that there were paranoid schizophrenics hiding under every rock.

Nietzsche says there is only one world, cruel and violent as it is.

Detective

I offer my services to those who want to recover their lives. Not a biographer who would fashion a single, continuous narrative to explain or dramatize someone's career, I am more akin to a detective offering items, evidence of their own lives. I find old love affairs, interview abandoned friends, discover the passing individual upon whose life my client may have made a profound impact without even realizing it ("He changed my life!"), scour city streets for enemies happy to air old grudges ("I could kill the bastard right now!"). Entire episodes that disappeared from a client's memory would be built up from ruins, whole stories abandoned or forgotten I reconstruct and offer to a client to do with it as he would, which was usually nothing more than hours of rueful contemplation over too much gin, although it could also lead to strange reunions, revived friendships, even lawsuits.

This is not an easy process. Certainly, it's not easy to find witnesses to someone's past, but it is often even more difficult for the client to accept the results, particularly since they often present unforeseen problems. Afterwards, many clients wish they had let sleeping dogs lie or had left so many proverbial stones unturned. The client may have thought he was merely a run-of-the-mill fool all of his life only to discover that he was a bona fide jerk, an ingrate in the eyes of companions who had long ago forgotten him or dismissed him as a creep. I always insert a clause in each contract protecting myself from unintended consequences (and I keep a psychiatrist on retainer for emergency referrals); even so, too often I would have to fend off irate customers who blame the messenger rather than the message.

I am often called upon by people who are accomplished or successful (after all, you need a little money to hire a professional to recover your past), although I work for nominal fees for those with large hearts and little cash. Not all clients are elderly, not all vain. I get my share of twentysomethings working sixty hours a week making millions inventing internet start-ups. Despite all the bullshit about the internet, they're disconnected—there's no worldwide web of the past—so they come to me, the human search engine to reclaim memories of the sixth grade or of high-school chums.

I make a point never to work for celebrities. The ruins of their lives are usually picked over pretty clean by tabloids or potential biographers; if anything, they need someone to rebury the past or at least to reinvent it. Besides, ordinary lives are interesting enough; real gems are waiting to be discovered: the insult or hurt harbored for years the client isn't aware of inflicting, the love affair long forgotten by the client but cherished forever by the lover; the discovery of a son the client doesn't know he's fathered.

Satan's Asshole

"Hey," Danny DeVito greeted the mailman, flinging his hand out in a perfunctory wave. The actor barely noticed the postman out of the corner of his eye as he reached into his mailbox with his other hand. But then he did a double take and froze when he glimpsed the ski mask over the guy's face, and in a flash the cold, stubby barrel of an Uzi was jammed against his nose.

He knew it was Gary, but he wouldn't let on for fear the disclosure would anger him. He didn't say anything while Gary rambled on incoherently.

"See, to get to heaven you got to go to hell, the very bottom of hell, and there's Satan, and he's there with his three mouths chewing on the world's biggest sinners, and what you got to do is crawl into Satan's asshole. That's right, the way to get to heaven is right through Satan's asshole! Can you believe it?"

DeVito eyed the gunman with a blank stare.

"Do you think I'm kidding or something, *motherfucker?*" Gary shouted.

"No, not at all," he replied as calmly as he could. "You're the one sticking an Uzi in my face, so I don't think you're joking. Not one bit."

Gary's eyes, outlined by holes in his ski mask, drilled into the actor, and he stared back. There was silence.

"Through Satan's asshole," DeVito whispered, eventually.

"Good," the deranged mailman spat back, "because I'm sure as fuck not making this up. This is Dante's idea—Dante's the one who went to hell, not me!"

Lenny

We had no idea what to do with the Lenny Schneider kid. He worked for us, and he was a quick learner and had a real keen way of selling the cartons of eggs and jars of preserves in the stand we kept on Montauk Highway outside the farm. He was friendly, affable, and the customers felt so good buying the eggs we would run out and have to import more of them from New Jersey—it was our little secret, and they were fresh, but not quite Long Island-farm fresh.

He was a good kid and a good worker, but he was just a hired hand, not a part of the family. We kind of got the feeling, though, that he felt that he really was family, that we were like the parents he never had—not that he was an orphan, but he did come from a broken, show-business family, Jewish too, and my wife said we probably made about as homey a place as he had ever lived in. It was a shame, but we weren't really aiming to adopt him or anything. He was just a hired hand, like I said.

When Lenny signed up for the Navy, we wished him well and saw him off. All these American boys were going off to fight the Nazis and the Japs, so it was the right thing to do, our duty to wish him well. But when he started sending us letters from his ship in the Mediterranean, from Anzio and other battles, writing up some pretty rough stories, some awful grisly things he had to see—how the dead bodies of soldiers bobbed up and down in the water by his ship all chalky and bloated. Well, we didn't know exactly what the right thing to do was, so we did the next best thing: we didn't do anything.

We never did answer his letters, and when he came back to Long Island after the war he was very warm and happy to see us, just like a kid coming home, but we kept our distance. "Hope to see you around," we said or something like that, something proper but real cool so he wouldn't get the wrong impression, wouldn't get some idea that we were like his mother and father, then we drove off in our truck.

He never did come back to see us, and we figured we had done the right thing by giving him the cold shoulder because it must have sunk in that he had the wrong idea about us.

We had just about forgotten about the Schneider kid, but then ten or so years later we were surprised to read in the newspaper that he had been arrested for being a dirty comic at one of those Greenwich Village beatnik nightclubs—he had changed his last name to Bruce, called himself Lenny Bruce, but we recognized his face in the photo. Like I said, we were surprised, but we also felt a lot of relief. After all, this kid turned out to be a bad apple, a real toilet mouth, and it was a good thing we didn't let him think we were like his second mom and dad. We knew then we did the right thing. Just think of all the trouble and all the shame we would have had to deal with if we had treated him like our own son.

FOUR

Dream

One night Alex dreamt that he was a woman. He was wearing a pink cashmere sweater and a blue cashmere skirt, just like his mother. The smooth, warm feel of the cashmere caressed him as he rubbed his hands over his breasts. In fact, he *was* his mother, and he woke up terrified and crying at the erotic confusion.

The next night he dreamt that he was standing in a large grassy field running from side to side as a tiny speck in the sky grew closer and closer. It was a bomb, and he knew that he was meant to catch the falling projectile. This should be frightening, he realized, yet he was strangely giddy, laughing as he ran back and forth across the field, tilting one way then the next, trying to position himself as the payload fell. Finally, he could see the torpedo shape, the stabilizer fins almost upon him, and he rushed underneath it, giggling, as it hurtled the last ten feet at fantastic speed. But just as the bomb was about to fall into his arms, he shot up in bed, awake.

He sat bewildered for a moment; then he laughed in a kind of delirium. What a relief that he hadn't actually caught the bomb, he sighed, although he also felt a little sad. This was confusing, this feeling good, refreshed even, that was mixed with a mild regret. But why should he feel this way? Amusement and regret for not catching a bomb?

Alex had had evocative, weird dreams before, of course. But having these two dreams back to back, one frightening, the other giddy when, if anything, they should have been the reverse—wearing the cashmere should have been a laugher, catching the bomb should have been a screamer—well, this was just too strange. I must be gay, he thought, except he didn't harbor any secret desires, at least none he knew of.

He decided to see Madame Zanco who perched in the front window of the first-floor flat of his building, the yellow of the neon palm flashing against her pale face as she sat on her crimson couch. He had never before gone to have the swarthy lady (she was a Gypsy, he supposed) peer at his palms or to have his Tarot cards read, but this seemed to be the right moment to consult an oracle.

"Hmm," the fortuneteller considered Alex's pair of dreams, eyeing both of his palms, then peering into his eyes. The way her gold earrings swayed from side to side reminded him of the way he ran from one end of the field to the other chasing the bomb, and he had to suppress an almost irrepressible chuckle. Then he became even more concerned: why would pendulant earrings make him laugh in the first place?

Finally, Madame Zanco stopped cogitating and spoke. "These are curious dreams, and they speak of what will come, no doubt."

"Yes?" he leaned towards her eagerly.

"Will you be afraid of what I tell you?" She dropped his hands.

"It depends—is it bad?"

"No, not really," she said, and then paused too long, as if mustering the courage to speak. "You are ready to have a child, that is all," she finally continued. "You will be the father of a son."

"A son? How can I have a son? *What—with my mother?* I'm not even married."

"Yes, married or not—or perhaps that will come first— no matter, you see, the message is clear; laughter and tears, it can be no other: a son. That is all, a son."

He stared at her in confusion, then alarm—which quickly turned to scorn when he realized he had actually consulted a fortuneteller instead of a shrink.

Ridiculous, he thought to himself.

"Not so ridiculous," Madame Zanco replied to his unspoken word. "Congratulations."

The Never-Ending Story
One never knows, do one?
From here to the Twelfth of Never is a long, long time
I never promised you a rose garden
Never the twain shall meet
Quoth the Raven, "Nevermore"
And I never, ever get sick at sea

Dear Boy,

The way I figured it, Jesus got a bum deal from his dad. What kind of a dad would abandon his own son when the kid was in trouble the way Jesus was? I could never understand it. What father would leave his only boy nailed up to a bunch of boards if he had the power to help? It doesn't seem right—how could Jesus' dad be God and act like such a shit? God is not supposed to be a shit, so I reckoned there was something wrong with the story, though it took me years before I could get to the bottom of the mystery.

Then one day it dawned on me: God wasn't really his father. Yeah, Jesus' dad was really Satan—and Jesus just told everyone his dad was God because he was embarrassed about who his dad really was and he wanted to make everyone feel good. I mean, Jesus was an OK guy who cared about people, and telling them that his dad was actually Satan wouldn't do anyone any good, so he told a lie—not a bad lie, just a white lie to make people happy. When he finally does get nailed up, and Jesus yells out, "Father, why hast Thou forsaken me?" that bastard Satan just ignored the whole thing, just went on drinking beer, watching TV, jerking off, just like nothing happened.

His dad really was a shit, it's just that the big shit that was his dad wasn't God. You understand, that's the difference. Otherwise, we'd be mad at God, which isn't right, but it's OK to be mad at Satan.

I imagine you often think of me like I was Satan. But if I forget you, if I abandon you in your time of need, if I treat you like dirt when you cry out, I can only wish that you'd be more like Jesus and keep the bad news about your real father to yourself and make up some lie.

Adieu

Never say Die
Never show them you're afraid
Never would have thought of it
Never say Never
Never heard from since
Never mind
Never speak unless spoken to
Never Again

Funny

"Wouldn't it be funny if all the air in the room suddenly went to one corner and we all suffocated?"

The four college girls huddled over the bed in the dorm room barely glancing at Jessica, and went on playing cards.

"Do you think I can throw up all these cards in the air and have them land in a pile ordered according to suit? Isn't entropy wonderful?"

"Jessica," sighed the dark-haired girl in t-shirt and shorts dealing the cards. "If you touch these cards one more time you'll get entropy shoved up your butt," she said, without turning her eyes from the deck.

None of the girls saw Jessica swing the baseball bat.

Joke

The nexus or nugget of difference which both links and separates the food-dirtying joke from the scatological or frankly coprophagous joke, in which feces are actually eaten or wildly flung about, is that in the food-dirtying joke it is the food which is being "dirtied" by the touch of sex, while in the scatological or coprophagous joke it is the victim or butt of the joke who is being dirtied by the touch of shit. Either as a food-dirtying or as a scatological joke, you can better understand why non-Christians consider the Christian communion—eating the body of God, which, of course, includes the rectum and other private parts—so scandalously funny.

Seeing is deceiving

Voice

I heard the muffled voice, a girl's voice, but I couldn't see anyone in the room. Silence. Then I heard it again, a kind of buzz or vibration.

After awhile it dawned on me that the muffled voice was coming from the wall itself.

I put my ear to the wall, then my hand, and I felt it bubble out slightly. "Mmmmry," I heard her say as if she were mumbling through a gag or yelling from a great distance.

The little girl was somehow embedded in the wall, buried between the plaster and the wallpaper, and the wallpaper bulged out faintly—the bump could barely be perceived—as she slid from one corner to the next, each time mumbling, "Mmmmry."

There was something else: an eerie, melancholy air that hung about the mutterer.

"Mary? Is that your name?"

The bulge shifted slightly up and down.

"Mary, what in the world is a nice young lady like you doing in that wall?"

You never had it so good

Patty Hearst

The world is Hostage in love with the Taker, and could Patty Hearst brainwash otherwise locked in a dark closet 56 days be otherwordly enough to light up the sky with LAPD? Speak to Patty Hearst, only bars on the window, so my sister can't climb out on the mansion roof, I will fail to leave an impression, Mom and Dad, a little rich bitch, FBI on the lawn the roof the nervous system, and now I will closet myself. My prison my "Patty Hearst" my fortress my God my flames. Strangely enough, as I was being bound, a great sense of relief swept over me.

Never enough

Dear Boy,
  Getting so drunk that you barf all over the couch and the living-room rug the way your buddy Michael did is no sweet delight of virtue. Such behavior does not set a good example for any of your friends, and nobody wants to asso-

ciate with a drunken fool. I for one don't want that dumb fuck Michael in my house ever again, and you don't want someone else's father to say the same of you.

And don't show your teeth when you smile. Really smart people don't crack up or guffaw or snort like a dog, and loud laughter is that sort of uncouth thing creeps do, so keep your mouth shut. When anyone really cool hears a little quip or a one-liner, he simply smiles, because real wit only needs a quiet sort of quiver or curl of the lips. Only buffoons who puke all over the living-room rug howl and shriek over reruns of I Love Lucy. Avoid movies that make you scream, whether comedies or horror flicks. Of course, I'm not a good example since I howled with laughter the first time I saw Richard Pryor do standup. Still, it's best to keep a poker face, a blank deadpan, and never let on what you think. The more you don't let on, the more people will respect you. Shut up, and they'll give you positions of power, they'll trust you, they'll line your palms with cash, no matter how scared or ignorant or stoned you really are. Keep your mouth shut and win.

Adieu

Mars Virus

Whether you like Harry or not, you have to give him credit: he clearly knows how to pick his nose.

Once he gets going, Harry's grey, greasy index finger would seem to gouge out his brains, reach through his skull to yank out his entire spinal cord. Other people just extract tiny balls of gummed up dust and mucous in cautious, furtive operations. Harry, on the other hand, reorders the entire molecular structure of his protoplasmic universe, while the other captives in the Mars Infection Cell all look on as collective witness.

Watching Harry is like sitting in Carnegie Hall, some fiddler sawing away at the cat guts, only this Paganini is plucking nose guts. The music seems just as sweet, and the performance just as brilliant, at least for this miserable, God-forsaken audience. And when he would plunge especially deep into his cranium, when he would seem to reach right through his nostril and into his very soul, the shackles attached to his wrists would rattle, and the hollow, creepy cell would echo with a kind of clanking music. Then our poor hearts would soar, filled with something akin to joy.

Harry was lucky he still had a nose to pick. He certainly had no ears.

Patty Hearst

Early reports characterized Patty Hearst as a beautiful, intelligent liberal, while in more recent reports I'm a comely girl who's been brainwashed by the SLA. Expropriated. Casualties could have been avoided if everyone in the bank had cooperated with the people's forces, I am a soldier in the people's army. Who are you? How do I know Regis Debray really wrote this note?

There's never any mess

Dear Boy,

 Half the people walking down the street are actually talking to themselves. Just get an old wallet or a TV remote and hold it to your mouth or stick some wax in your ear and dangle a wire and you too can rant and rave, tell the bastards to get lost while you promenade down the boulevard, no questions asked. And it is good to talk to your self, real salubrious. The older you get, the more arguments you have—and lose—with yourself, so keep the wallet handy. Otherwise, they might think you're crazy talking to yourself. People see someone on a bus crying by his lonesome and they think, "Oh, something terrible must have happened, poor thing, a death in the family, such a

tragedy." But people see someone on a
bus laughing to himself, quietly giggling or loudly quivering with guffaws,
and they think, "Some loony-toons
fruitcake just escaped the nuthouse,
lock the sonovabitch up!" So argue and
rant, sputter and fume, giggle and
snort, just so long as you keep something to your ear that looks like a
cell phone, and you're protected, a
bona fide member of consumer communication. Even an old potato or a fist
would do, in a pinch. What else are
these damn fools doing but yapping to
themselves, anyway? Who else would want
to talk with them?

Adieu

> If you love it enough, anything will talk to you.
> If it dislikes you enough, it will never shut up.

Patty Hearst

*Kind of like the pet chicken on the farm that's me—when it comes
time to kill it for Sunday dinner no one really wants to die in the
shootout. Join them or die, you can go home if you want to,
really, so staying alive one day at a time and if the FBI stormed
the place I would die in the shootout like Cujo Gelina Gabi Zoya
Fahizah and then Teko and Yolanda whom I hate and Cinque
Mtume, shifting the blindfold to the top of my head peeking*

through the blindfold conducting my own surveillance, looking out the top of the blindfold, door can't close all the way, I know too much, besides paranoia must be contagious. "Your pig father has psychics don't think of any psychics right now don't communicate with them. You can fuck any man in the cell you want to or any woman but don't communicate with psychics." Dressed like a combat soldier for the picture Cin christened me with my revolutionary name, Tania, saying they will automate the entire industrial state to the point that in five years all they need will be a small class of button pushers and now is the time for removal of expendable excess which is The People but better yet now the rich girl also expendable excess "Tania." Unreal, myself on TV robbing my best friend's father's bank, I sensed that Tania had, in fact, crossed over some sharp line of demarcation, not me, not really, I am "Patty Hearst" my conversion my closet. "You give the people hope you must stay," Cin said, "They believe in you, you must stay, you must fight on." Many meanings like psychic multiplication tables of "Patty Hearst" keep me alive: "Ask me to do anything ask me to rob a bank with you but don't ask me to go to a movie theater and get arrested while watching Citizen Kane."

Dear Boy,

So your boss is an asshole. You're not the first one to discover this. So a secretary quit after just one day, and the other one walked out after two weeks, all because he's an obsessive jerk who won't let people do their jobs. Just remember that sometimes it pays to have a job low down on the totem pole like yours because all you

do is follow orders and you're not supposed to think, which means your boss
won't have much chance to butt in.
Enjoy being invisible, and watch everyone else get burnt, but don't let the
bastards touch your brains.

Once I operated printing presses at
Lin Litho, tried to bring the union in
with some other people: biggest non-
union shop in town. I was running 11X17
newsletters for Bank of America at top
speed, the paper flying out, when the
supervisor comes by and yells "Faster!"
Times like that I would have killed the
worm—if I could've stopped laughing at
the asshole long enough. All of us in
the basement, press operators, graphic
artists, even the ethnic Chinese from
Vietnam in the bindery terrified of the
INS, all would tilt towards the union
because the boss upstairs—a steely
Chinese matriarch—ran roughshod over
everyone.

Then someone in management—maybe that
Harvard snob who handled customer relations with corporate clients—would bring
boxes of donuts down to the press room
in the basement. Suddenly people in the
shop wouldn't be so pissed: all anger
dissolved into the silvery glaze of the
donut. Donuts were literally sugar bul-
lets. Or we'd be forced to work overtime,
so they would bring down McDonald,s for

dinner and scowls turned to smiles. "Hey, they ain't so bad." That's all it took to bribe some people: a goddamn donut, a sloppy Big Mac. I'm no St. Francis, I know bribes have their say, but I was amazed at how easy it was, how little it took to snooker people.

So think about it: do you want to be one of those dumb fucks who takes the donut and thinks, "Aw, the boss ain't so bad," even though in a hundred other ways you're getting screwed? I wouldn't suggest that you refuse the donut, of course, since it'll just go to waste and you do not want to offend by turning down a gift. But what you want to do is take the oozing donut, chomp down on the greasy burger, enjoy anything and everything you can get your hands on, and then thank the bastards—but KEEP YOUR BRAINS! Take the bribe, just don't obey it. Is that so hard?

Adieu

The dot extends into a vertical line
which indicates we are either on the way up
or on the way down,
but never quite here.

Patty Hearst

That strange look, Cinque he did not quite say he was descended from God or instructed by him, strange beyond his usual strangeness, secrets from some mystical world beyond our understanding, Christ talking to his disciples the United Symbionese Nation he was the founder and father of a new nation. He knocked on doors: "Hello, I'm Field Marshal Cinque of the SLA" and people would actually help, so Cin is right—the people do support us. Food from two Black Muslim families the little girl loved Cin his code name Jesus. "When are we going to see Jesus again?" Helicopters over Hunters Point, fascist pigs pursuing black excess but then Tania and the other eight white comrades put on burnt cork blackface, pigs never imagine us Black, and Cinque puts on a dress, dressed up as a buxom, swishing woman, escape to new safehouse and no one could spot us. "The last time I saw Jesus he looked like a woman."

Never in a thousand years

Donation

"Your good deed, your donation will not go unnoticed. More good deeds like this, sir, and cancer will be cured. Your charity will be added to your soul's account, your credit for the afterlife."

"Credit for the afterlife? Like a bar tab? I don't want an afterlife, not even one in heaven. One life is enough, I don't need one after it. Is this some kind of a joke? Do I have to live forever, trapped without a body?"

Silence.

"Why can't I stay dead?"

Silence.

"Give me my fucking donation back!"

"So, exactly what is the Consumer Confidence Index?"

Mars Virus

I had returned early from Mars with the express purpose of seeing Rocamora's *Patty Hearst*. The beginning of the celebrated "Escape to the New Safehouse" duet in Act Three, with Patty and her white comrades in blackface, while Cinque is decked out in a wig and a dress—it was exquisite. "No Fascist Insect dreams to see me Black/Now fear can never turn Love's Tania back," sang Maria Cameron as Patty. Her soprano soared against the rich baritone of Lafcadio Bloom's Cinque: "No Fascist Insect dreams to see me in a dress—"

Suddenly my Genital Communicator threw up an emergency hologram.

It was Bullock, commander of the Mars Infection Cell. There had been a riot, and several prisoners had lost additional body parts. One had escaped, dangerous and armed with T.E.E.T.H. Would I come. Quickly.

The image vanished as wild applause filled the hall. I had missed almost the entire duet.

I reattached my GC, zipped up my fly, and sighed. Opera has no place on such a dangerous planet as Earth.

Outside, a Transport was already waiting for me, throbbing at the curb.

It's not as if God spoke to you
and promised that you would found a nation
as plentiful as the stars
if you would only kill your own son

FIVE

This, then, is where our story begins.

Red Phone

When they finally put Erich Mielke in Moabit prison he was an old man in his eighties. For decades the chief of the feared East German secret police known as the Stasi, Mielke was put on trial for a crime in the 1930s. He was convicted for the political assassination of two policemen in retaliation for the murder of Communists, and not for any misdeeds during the Communist regime itself. Luckily for the prosecutors, he could be accused of the failures of the Weimar Republic and they could avoid any messy Hitler-Stalin complications.

The old man's spirits were very low, and the guards worried about his morale. Already morose, he grew increasingly despondent, and they were afraid he would fall ill, even die. If he died on them it would be very messy, and he needed to live at least long enough for the trial.

After some thought, the prison guards put a red telephone in his cell, the thick, bulky kind that he had enjoyed as a member of the Politburo.

Mielke seemed to scoff at first. The red phone was not connected to the outside world, not even to the guards. But after a short time he began to pick up the bright red receiver and speak into it. More and more Mielke began dialing, cradling the receiver to his ear, conducting imaginary conversations, conferring with phantom subordinates, issuing orders—almost like the old days.

Soon the old man brightened up.

My dream ended, and I became confused.
My dream resumed, and my eyes opened.

Delete.

Bedtime Story

Barney told me yesterday that they were letting me go, and I don't know how you tell a kid her pop is a flop—yet again.

I didn't want to tell Missy that I was fired, but I knew I would anyway.

I thought I was hot, coming up with ideas with real legs, but no one else thought so.

Our client was some local environmental protection agency, and they needed some PR buffing of their image.

So I suggested a parody message campaign, "Got Sludge," with celebrities like Madonna drinking a glass of water with a brown "milk" mustache, or "Got Smog?" and have dirt smeared around a kid's face, you know, a take-off on the hit "Got Milk" campaign.

That got nowhere.

Then I dreamt up another take-off: "A Waste is a Terrible Thing to Mind."

The EPA rep just gave me a strange, anguished look, "A waste is a what?"

"You know, like the United Negro College Fund?"

"A Waste is a Terrible Thing to Mind?" Missy repeated when I went to tuck her in after *Goodnight Moon*.

I told Missy I got canned like it was a bedtime story, nothing to worry about. Just a fairy tale—and tomorrow will bring the happy ending.

"Yeah, Missy, that was it."

"Pop, that's like the perfect slogan for you," she said, as I pulled the covers up to her chin. "You mind everyone else's waste, but they don't mind you. They don't give you credit for picking up all their garbage."

The sweet smile she gave me just then was worth getting fired from a million jobs.

The next morning I robbed my first bank.

> Here is Body, but not Flesh.
>> The Soul sees, but not with Eyes.
> "One Mimesis with Fantasia," she elects,
>>> "But hold the French fries."

Officer's Diary

Sorsagon, Bicol Region, Philippines
17 July, 1901

A strange occurrence outside Sorsagon, so uncanny I have not yet made a report to headquarters in Manila.

Frankly, I don't know if I ever will.

Several fishermen in agitated state brought in a small boy, perhaps nine or ten. The boy appeared Anglo-Saxon or at least white, wearing brightly colored shoes made of a strange substance, denim trousers and a thin blue collarless shirt with a brushstroke symbol that looked like an Australian boomerang imprinted on its breast. On his head was a cap, very much like a baseball cap, but with that same white brushstroke symbol over its brim. The fishermen chattered all at once in the local Bicol dialect, but one or two could speak Spanish, and from them I was able to piece together their story.

Several of them were walking to the shore after that morning's torrential downpour when they spotted a pair of legs sticking out from the ground. They leaped back in fright. Then they noticed that the legs wriggled and, thinking some freak accident had occurred that had buried someone head first in mud, they raced over and pulled the legs out of the soft soil to discover that the limbs belonged to a little boy. The boy spit out dirt and blew his nose, but otherwise he seemed fine.

The boy's strange arrival, not to mention his white skin, caused great consternation and a terrible sense of dread. They poked him, squeezed his arms, determined that he appeared real enough, but they could not understand how someone, especially someone as out of place as a white boy, could be found in such a bizarre position. Soon panic spread among the fishermen, some thinking that the boy was an *asuang*, some kind of a demon. Most such demons take the form of a beautiful woman, a kind of succubus, who comes to drain the life out of some unwitting man seduced by the demon's wiles, but it was not unthinkable that an *asuang* could also take the form of a small boy. One insisted he was the boy Jesus. Others cried out that, demon or Jesus, the *Americanos* would blame them for hurting a white boy, might even accuse them of being insurgents and kill them all, and they better take the child to the soldiers or there would be untold bloody consequences.

So with much shouting and signs of alarm, they came to my tent, bringing the boy, who seemed as bewildered as they, in tow.

The boy did not respond to the native dialect of the Filipinos, so I tried speaking to him in Spanish.

I asked who he was, where he came from, and other such questions.

When he heard me speak he grinned and replied, with great vigor, "*La vida loca!*"

The fishermen gasped at the boy's declaration.

The boy thought for a moment, then added, "*Hasta la vista*, baby."

"*Como se llama?*" I asked him.

"That's all the Spanish I know—Ricky Martin and The Terminator," he went on in a perfect American accent. "But I can—"

His talk was cut off, interrupted by the incredible fact that he suddenly and swiftly began to sink into the ground. I was stunned, and before I could even reach out to him he had slipped deep into the soil right before my very eyes. How could Headquarters believe anything so preposterous? But as surely as the earth opened up to swallow Kora, the boy was gone.

The fishermen began to scream and run away in terror, some shouting, "*La vida loca! La vida loca!*"

Dear Boy,
    When you read this I will be dead, of course.

    I made arrangements before the cancer made clear thinking impossible to have this delivered to you. Mark Twain thought only the dead could tell the truth, but even now that I'm dead I'm not sure that I won't lie. I'll try not to.

This is the first of many communications you will receive from me. I have constructed a kind of ghost of myself, and I have every intention of haunting you. I have no desire to inspire fear, only presence.

Arrangements have been made with various entities to deliver mail, send emails, deliver videos, produce paid messages on radio, publish articles, deploy singing messengers, mimes, acrobats—in short, to draw upon every means or medium of communication in order to send you messages from the dead on a regular basis. I am still arranging for various rock 'n roll and hip-hop artists to convey their musical interpretations of messages from me. At this writing I am not sure if this effort will be a success. Nonetheless, you can anticipate Madonna or some other pop star releasing "Dead Dad" or some such title some time or other, just as you may one day see a remake of the Hollywood movie <u>Ghost Dad</u>, with maybe Harvey Keitel instead of Bill Cosby playing me.

Messages will come at random times. Perhaps years will pass before you receive the next one. Nevertheless, I have arranged for communications to be sent to you for at least forty years.

Most messages will have nothing profound to say. Just the fact that a message from your dead father is delivered is enough.

I will never leave you.

Adieu

Dirty Limerick

The nipples of Sarah Sarong,
When excited, are twelve inches long. . .

It was hopeless—he knew he could never write a dirty limerick to save his life. He put on his jacket and slowly walked out of the office.

"Wait," he heard Susan call after him, his hand on the cool brass of the doorknob. "Try this: *There once was a girl from Kentucky / Who sometimes would feel awfully fucky . . .*" She looked after him plaintively, her eyes filled with hope and panic and yearning.

"*So Bob made her gong bong / With the end of his dong,*" she paused expectantly, waiting for him to supply the last line.

Bob only smiled and shook his head slowly and quietly shut the door behind him.

"*AND THERE AIN'T NO SONOVABITCH MORE LUCKY!*" Susan screamed after him—and then she burst out into bitter tears.

> He that sitteth in the heavens shall laugh:
> the Lord shall hold them in derision.

Satan's Asshole

What caught her eye was the odd sight of the man in a ski mask in the hot Malibu afternoon, then the glint of the gun against the head of the other short, balding man. It was all so brief, such a quick glance, that it hadn't quite registered, so she turned her head to get a better look as she drove down the Pacific Coast Highway, and it was at that point that she lost control of her Toyota, rolled over twice, slammed into a Grand Cherokee coming the other way, then came to rest with her two front wheels dangling over the edge of a cliff above the Pacific Ocean.

When she came out of the coma she couldn't remember her name or anything else about herself. Oddly, only that brief flash before the accident had lodged firmly in her memory: the ski mask, the glint, the short balding man. Everything before or after was blank.

She told the police what she thought she had witnessed, though they never did find any ski mask or gun or short balding man or any kind of wrongdoing, and she became convinced that it was a dream. Her mind was playing cruel tricks, toying with her to remember a moment that hadn't even happened in order to dam up the torrent of true recollections. Either that, or the earth had simply swallowed up the two.

In a few days she was well enough to sit up in bed and watch TV, and she would flip the remote from channel to channel hoping to discover something about herself in some old situation comedy. The newscasters talked about her and showed photos of people who were said to be her father and her brother. Both of them were on their way from Chicago. She studied their faces, but they were strangers to her now, nothing but blanks, and when they announced her own name she didn't recognize it.

HILTON OBENZINGER

Then she channel surfed to a movie.

"Oh, that's a funny one," the nurse kibitzed, as she came in to take her blood pressure. "*Throw Mama From the Train*—about a writer who gets roped into killing someone's mother."

Suddenly her heart shot up into her mouth, and the amnesiac let out a scream.

"That's him! That's him!" she gasped, jabbing her finger at the TV.

"That's who?"

"That's the man I saw! *That's him! That's the man with the gun to his head!*"

The nurse squinted up at the screen. "Which is the one? Danny DeVito or Billy Crystal?"

> The center is everywhere, the circumference is gone,
> So she expected no less of his dong.
> But he told her quite happily,
> "Mine's called Metonomy,"
> And he sucked up her cunt with aplomb.

Officer's Diary

Sorsagon, Bicol Region, Philippines
4 September, 1901

A procession was organized by the new "La Vida Loca" Santo Niño cult a few months after the holy boy's appearance. Ever since Magellan brought his first Papist doll of the baby Jesus to these islands, the Filipinos have wedded their irrepressible pagan instincts to the Church's pious frauds, making the Santo Niño cults extremely popular. These Santo Niño idols, elaborately carved wooden dolls with gaudy royal robes and little golden crowns, are paraded in the natives' religious processionals, adored as if divine.

Now the new cult had carved the white features of the boy who they said had fallen from heaven and landed headfirst in the beach near Sorsagan. They dug him out of the sand, and on his head they found the baseball cap with its strange brushstroke symbol, the same as what was painted on his blue shirt. Most impressive of all were the doll's shoes, a kind of white and blue papier-mâché of the odd rubbery-looking footwear he wore that day of his first advent. There had been some thought about making banners with the boomerang brushstroke symbol, but after consultation with the Church the decision came about to display what had become a new sacred symbol only on the Santo Niño doll itself and preserve the Cross as the sole symbol of the Church.

"*La Vida Loca!*" the procession chanted with great joy between Hail Marys.

The new cult believed that their little part of the Philippine Islands had been visited by an incarnation of the boy Jesus. He had fallen from the sky, and he would return someday to Sorsagon to redeem his children, which filled them all with gladness and a humbling sense of God's will. A vision would overcome them of the brushstroke symbol filling the entire world to hasten the boy's final advent, at which point the second slogan, "*Hasta la vista, baby!*" would rise from their throats, the anticipation was so great.

"*La Vida Loca*," they all chanted again. Some believed the phrase from the boy's own lips was a condemnation of sinfulness.

"*La Vida Loca!*" Others reckoned it was a lament, an expression of mercy at mankind's fallen state.

"La Vida Loca!" A few surmised that it spoke of things to come, of a "crazy" time of joy and peace.

Whatever the interpretation, they knew that from now until the mystery is revealed at the end of time those words would be an inseparable part of their lives.

"If your sacred mountain is somewhere inside your head,"

the Indian asked,

"then where do you go to learn how to pray?"

Mars Virus

Mars was not the origin of the virus but only the last transit point before it entered Earth Systems.

The virus attacks the implanted nanoneurocybersomatic interlink—nanolink for short—and irreparably alters the cell-to-silicon Boolean Exchange.

The nanolink communication and computer system has been implanted in human brains for nearly a century, and never had such an invasive software worm caused so much havoc. Victims of previous viruses would hear disturbing voices as if they were actual calls from other nanolinks. No different than typical telepathic conversations, the voices would order infected receivers to do strange, unspeakable things. But with a simple schizometric reading the malfunction would be identified, the alien program would be quickly deleted, and the nanolink consumer would resume normal exchange.

This bug is different. When it strikes, the virus crosses synaptic boundaries, turning smooth analog biodeliveries into digitized spurts of DNA. Removing the nanolink implant does not help. Within moments of entering the biosystem the virus creates its own platform.

Once flesh is digitized, the body can then produce multiple ones and zeros at its narrowest points, even if combinations of the most unlikely odds. Infection can be dormant, unnoticed, until the random array of multiple zeros and ones suddenly results in some limb or other extremity turning translucent, cutting itself off from the rest of the protoplasmic file and, quite literally, falling off. This is why victims of the Mars virus lose their body parts, extremities like ears, noses, fingers, toes, legs, arms, all because the most improbable Boolean combination across the narrowest connecting point could dissolve all fleshly bonds. Penises and testicles are regularly dropped by men, while women typically lose their breasts within days of contracting the disease. In advanced cases, the rectum drops off along with shredded intestines.

Some of the worst victims have ended up without limbs, literally basket cases, in just seconds, all because the worst odds imaginable resulted in simultaneous amputations.

Janey Jimenez, Patty Hearst's Guard

Third woman first Chicana U.S. Marshall and first day of work after one hour they tell me, "Janey, take Patty Hearst to the hospital," maybe to show off how liberal they are or to make me crash and burn with the rich kid, I don't know. Wispy figure short-cut hair shapeless tangle, battered corduroys too baggy no bra bright red sweater outlines of small childlike breasts. I told her to stand with her legs well apart, spread out her arms, standard frisk, emptying her pockets, around the neck, from the back, up and down the arms, over ribs, breast, waistline, finally down the buttocks and legs, into the crotch, and we went to the gynecologist at Stanford, his hand up her vagina with her writhing and shrieking, and I thought: Rape victim.

Threats and more threats: I was a whore picked up on the streets and I was so nice to Patty because I was probably in on the whole anti-Establishment conspiracy, as a Chicana I had my own reasons for joining the SLA, then others threatened me because I was a Pig and threatened her because she was a traitor to the Revolution and I told her she had to follow my orders, otherwise we could both be killed, some Lee Harvey Oswald or Jack Ruby outside the Federal Building.

Once she understood she grew comfortable in my hands.

She began to relax when she realized I was in control.

One letter said I was doing even more than Angie Dickinson to improve the image of female law officers and would I marry him.

Only the city I am about to leave is holy.

Satan's Asshole

In the dim gray light I could see the outlines of huge stone blocks and columns artfully shaped and carved despite their wrecked condition amid the usual igneous outcrops and random chunks beneath the surface world. I could spot a group of soldiers or guards even more shadowy than the rest of the ruins, a few scanning the rubble with binoculars, most lounging, cleaning their weapons, and in the back, behind some blasted and crushed walls, I could hear the sound of children's laughter and mothers calling after them.

What a domestic scene. Yet the better part of caution meant I kept out of sight as I peered over a boulder. After all, the soldiers, dressed in tunics and old camouflage outfits, had swords and spears and even a few old carbines, so I had no desire to startle them.

"What a motley crowd. Who are these people?" I asked Danny DeVito.

"They are the rebels who rose up against Moses," he replied. "Kora complained that the laws were too burdensome and the common people would be ruined by them."

"So?"

"So, what do you think?" my guide snapped back. "Moses asked the Lord to open the mouth of the earth and swallow Kora's followers and their families whole. The Lord double checked, and he asked Moses if he was really, absolutely sure, and Moses said he was, so the Lord shrugged and did as the prophet requested, which was to have the earth swallow up Kora and his followers in a single gulp. But as they were sliding down earth's open gullet some of the rebels repented and swore loyalty to Moses. These pathetic wretches cried out for mercy, and the Lord heard them. The Lord took a sidelong glance at Moses, looking for a sign he had relented, but the hardass wouldn't even flinch, and so down they went to the underworld with all the rest.

"But when many years later the Temple was destroyed by the Romans, and its columns and thick walls all torn down and thrown into the bowels of the earth, the Lord remembered these repentant rebels and He appointed them to be the guardians of the Temple's portals, and they and their families were brought to this place not far from the surface.

The former rebels eagerly took up their posts, and they calculated that when the Temple would be restored, when its columns and stone blocks would be called back up to the surface, they would hitch a ride along with the rubble, returning to the world of sunlight, and there they would continue as loyal guardians of the sacred portals."

"But how long will they have to wait? When will the Lord return the stones of the Temple to the surface?"

"Are you kidding?" Danny DeVito snorted. "Haven't you been down here long enough to know?"

Janey Jimenez, Patty Hearst's Guard

"I don't know what's happening, nobody tells me, I just get my orders, I feel like an outcast, that I belong with you. Hell, I'm the prisoner and not Patty Hearst!"

Nobody lets Janey Jimenez know what's going on.

Whichever way Patty turns she's trapped, and I'm trapped with her. Once a car backfired and with split-second reflex I rolled her to the ground, laughing afterwards. I had the sensation of watching a doomed bull in the correo, so I watched, alarmed, the jury sequestered for six and a half weeks, monitored, watched, captured too.

Guilty, guilty. She was guilty for being a woman, for allowing herself to be defiled, fucked by her captors, fucked by a Black man, guilty for failing to die, for not moving into the world of shades, for becoming a symbol or failing to become one, becoming Tania or failing to become Tania, making the mistake of staying alive, becoming a roadblock, a hindrance, guilty for being born a Hearst, and the public doesn't like seeing a rich bitch getting away with anything, no Queen of the SLA. Dead she would be free, and I was there to protect her, to keep her from becoming free.

My *father left but then one night he knocked on the door at 1AM "I want to see the children I have something I must tell them all of them," and my mother said come back at a decent hour footsteps trailed away and he came back next morning but when he was crossing the street he was hit by a car. Just like that. A week later, his message still undelivered, he was dead. So I see Patty with her family, and I know she never meant those things she said over the radio.*

Patty never wanted to see Citizen Kane, and she'd get mad if you suggested that she should.

Curriculum Vitae

The office was just a block from the train station in San Mateo. I opened the door, and the room looked about the size of a large closet. There was a desk with an IBM Selectric, two chairs, and a stack of paper. No windows, just blank walls, except for a photo of the Eiffel Tower. Why the Eiffel Tower?

I shut off the lights and sat in the darkness of the closet for hours, scribbling.

The phone rang. I jumped up, my heart pounding. Someone asking for information about getting his résumé written up. I tried to sound professional, efficient, knowledgeable. Career Objective. Curriculum Vitae. Education. Experience. References.

He hung up.

No windows. I sat, the walls moving closer. This is what my life as a writer had become: dressing up people's self-images in a dark closet, making them sound classier or more legit or phonier for the job mill. Not even paid by the hour but by piecework, résumé by résumé. I was supposed to sell them the gussied up, expanded version, push the rag paper, 11x17 folded over, make more money. I could hardly breathe.

When noon came I got up and turned the lights on, standing dazed before the picture of the Eiffel Tower. I ripped it off the wall, slid it under my arm, locked the door, and took the next train back to San Francisco.

When I got home I put the key in an envelope with a note on a slip of paper "Abandon All Hope Who Enter Here" and mailed it back to the main office across the street from the military cemetery in San Bruno.

SIX

Family Pictures

Kwame had found the metal box in a pile of junk left beside garbage cans on the sidewalk. It had a metallic, aluminum color and a rectangular, shallow shape, and when he pulled the little latch and opened the lid he found neat rows of colored slides, each carefully placed in a slot, a hundred or more. No one noticed—besides, it was left as rubbish—so he took the box home, thinking it would prove very useful for holding his own slides.

But before he replaced them with his own, he decided to take a look at the old slides, loading them one by one into a handheld viewer. A family story revealed itself, a collection dating back to the early sixties and moving through, what seemed by the fashions, to the late seventies or early eighties. He noted the standard, time-worn poses—mom and dad waving on the stoop of a suburban home, perhaps grandma was the older woman awkwardly peering into the camera, clearly a son and a daughter, at first making faces, then growing up and gracefully looping their arms around their parents' sagging shoulders in protective gestures— typical smiles, scenes of birthday parties, vacations in Yosemite and unidentifiable beaches, even a row of slides from Paris with mom and dad squinting into the sun in front of the Eiffel Tower, kids growing up, graduations, all the rituals and passages of domestic life, a typical white family. Other than a shot of the son and daughter standing with Danny DeVito between them against some greenery, the slides were emphatically, boringly ordinary.

Although Kwame wanted to use the box for his own slides, when he tried to toss the old slides into the garbage he was held back in mid swing. He could not throw away the family collection and he could not remove their splendid boringness from their aluminum casket. Had they decided to travel as a family to Paris only to perish every one in the airplane crash that had just flooded the news? Had the parents grown as old and faded as the slides until finally they had passed away? But why would their children throw away all the slides? The scenes were boring, of course, but had the children no nostalgia, no sentiment? The slides were duplicates, he reassured himself, refusing to believe that the children would dump the evidence of their parents' lives, and he invented increasingly elaborate stories to go along with the commonplace poses. The slides affected Kwame the way pictures of doomed Jews rounded up by the Nazis staring into some German camera haunted him, or the way photos of lynched Black men dangling from the noose spoke to him of unimaginable terror. Speculations of lives and feelings, fear and courage, each life just a flicker, soon forgotten by all. He knew what he was entertaining was a cliché—something akin to the "All is Vanity" proposition—but he hoped each time that he fondled the small squares of someone else's memory that a deeper something would reach out to him.

He tried to resist making up tales or names for all the players in his little drama. But each time he ran the slides through the projector his mind filled with competing scenarios. Why, suddenly, was the son missing from the sequence of photos? Did he fight with his father over his decision to marry the Chinese girl who appeared with him in just one picture? What brought even so briefly Danny DeVito into their lives? The sorrow in the parents' faces— did that mean the son had died, crushed in a car wreck, and they forever mourned their loss? No photo of the funeral? The daughter, with wavy auburn hair, deeply lined face, and somber expression, standing alone with her parents year after year—why didn't she marry? Was she keeping her lesbian lover secret from her anguished parents? Why did the lines in her face grow deeper? What did the father or the mother do for a living? Was he a civil engineer? Did she sell skirts and blouses in a small boutique? He did not look like a gangster, and she did not possess the air of a whorehouse madame—but perhaps looks deceive, and they were really crude, low-life types, their bland, middle-class exteriors masking their rotting souls.

Kwame never did put his own slides in the box, but kept the collection, for what reason he could never say. Probably a form of voyeurism, and he would admonish himself. Twice he masturbated with the wavy auburn hair of the youthful daughter before his eyes, a perversity close to necrophilia, he surmised. But there the family album remained tucked away amidst his own collections of memorabilia in the garage, and once a year or so he would fish out the slides and again consider their mysteries.

And there the matter rested. That is, until a few years later Kwame, literally, stumbled upon the daughter.

There was no question in his mind that it was her. He was shopping downtown when she pushed her way through the revolving doors of Macy's and collided directly into him, a clatter of cleaning implements hanging from her oversized yellow slicker. He recognized her immediately. She was older, of course, and oddly decked out in that outfitted yellow slicker, the kind that children wear, even though the weather was dry. Yet there was no doubt about it: the same wavy auburn hair, although now flecked with gray, the same deeply-lined face, only deeper, wrinkled even, and an expression just as somber as the person in the slides, despite the queer get-up.

Kwame turned after her after they collected themselves and exchanged mumbled pardons. He put his hand on her shoulder as she turned to go.

"Excuse me, but I believe I have your family's slides. Someone must have thrown them—" he blurted out, his eyes wide in disbelief.

She whirled around, glimpsing the Black man who seemed to be attacking her, and from within the depths of that odd yellow slicker she let loose a bloodcurdling shriek.

Fail Safe
Systems Failure
Fortunate Fall

Baseball

"I don't *need* aggravation. *I just want an orgasm and then to go to sleep.*"

The usual bullshit you overhear in bars. Real estate agents, a local DJ at the easy music station, secretaries, businessmen, the regulars.

"Whaddaya mean I'm not giving her three kids enough space? She can take her three kids and I can tell you up what kind of space she can shove 'em."

Then he caught the name "Marv Throneberry" at the far end, and he perked up.

It was a geezer wearing one of those cracked mahogany suntans he noticed all well-preserved Senior Citizens in Miami sport. A well-worn Marlins baseball cap perched on his head as he told his story to the codger fingering a beer beside him.

Ryan cocked his head to hear the rest.

"It was maybe the first or second year the Mets got the franchise," the old fan went on. "And they were playing in the Polo Grounds before they built Shea Stadium."

Ryan knew that time well. He would often sit in the Polo Grounds' upper deck in high school, a loyal fan. He knew the Mets was the worst team imaginable, even with Stan Musial and Willie Mays on their last legs and with Casey Stengel managing, but he loved them.

Ryan wasn't the only one—as the Mets scudded along the cellar of the National League, New Yorkers took them to their hearts. They lost games in dazzling, bumbling style, and with great regularity, but people began to call them the "Amazing Mets" because of the way they would suddenly, seemingly out of nowhere, rise up and play stunning ball, trounce the league leader, come from behind in the ninth inning, pull off breathtaking double plays, before they would slip back into such spectacular mediocrity you had no idea they could have ever accomplished such amazing feats.

"They called him Marvelous Marv because he was so terrible, one of the worst ball players ever," the geezer continued, "but then he would do something completely tremendous, like hit a homerun or he'd catch a long fly against the wall and he became, you know, *Marvelous* . . ."

The elderly gentleman told his story of how he watched Marvelous Marv hit a triple but get called out because he didn't touch first base. When Casey Stengel got up to protest the call, the umpire told him Marv hadn't stepped on second either.

Ryan drifted into his own recollections, the time Marv Throneberry, playing right field in the Polo Grounds, ran in for a shallow fly ball. It was a tough play but not an impossible one, the kind of play any major league ballplayer could pull off with not much effort. Marv came running in, arm extended, glove reaching out. He looked like he was going to make it, and Ryan stood up with everyone else in the stadium wondering if Marvelous Marv would.

Then it happened. Maybe the outfield grass was slick from the showers earlier or probably it was just Marv's luck, but he suddenly slipped, his feet flying up in the air, and he flopped on his back like Keystone Kops. A split second later the ball landed right on his belly, plop, and gently rolled off like a slow motion movie.

"Yeah, Marvelous Marv," Ryan chuckled to himself. "He knew how to turn failure into an art form."

"So, get this," the oldtimer's voice intruded. "What do you think when I find out he owns the next condo?"

If I slip and start writing of God,
it seems embarrassing, horribly embarrassing.
All of this was supposed to have been over a long time ago.

Our Lady of Shit

Think about the Eiffel Tower, the monstrous Eiffel Tower. They called it a hole-riddled suppository, it's a fortress and it's lace, slim as a hat pin, so you wonder what got into their heads— art and useless—but an obscene monument to engineers or what have you and you know Eiffel designed the steel frame that Bartholdi or whoever built it draped the Statue of Liberty on top of, you know that long wavy dress, so Eiffel did all those girders inside and remember that the next time you spiral around and around climbing up the Statue of Liberty you're really climbing up the lady's dress right up her privates, so Eiffel's tower is not the big phallic symbol they like to talk about—no, no—his tower is really a naked lady sticking up in the middle of Paris, a kind of useless steel pornography. In fact most of those buildings they take for big male members are nothing but husky women, for example what about that Empire State Building just look at it it's just like a towering I don't know what, a towering Kim Basinger or Lauren Bacall, some movie star with big shoulders. Kind of opens your eyes don't it?

Archaeology

Dr. Kendricks took the brush to the spot of reddish textile and steadily swept the sand back. Up until now the dig was disappointing, and winter would soon be upon them, forcing them to clear off the mountaintop. But bit by bit the mummy revealed itself. Maybe ten or eleven years old, the child was bound tightly, knees up to the chest, prepared in the usual fashion for the Inca sacrifice to the mountain god.

The mummy looked like all the other Inca child sacrifices Dr. Kendricks had excavated, except for the odd fact that what looked very much like a blue baseball cap embellished with Nike's swoosh logo was squashed onto the child's head.

"Damn looters!" he fumed. But then he realized that grave robbers could not have preceded him to tamper with the site. Other than the apparent addition of the hat, the mummy had lain undisturbed, frozen in the mountaintop's permafrost.

And when he received the report from the lab after he sent fibers to be analyzed, he knew his life would be changed forever. The lab concluded that the baseball cap

and the tunic were from the same time period, even the
faded, threadbare label inside the cap.

The tunic and the cap were both over 700 years old!

Dear Boy,
  When I got the report that it might
be cancer but I would have to take some
tests to find out for sure, you can bet
I went through a lot of changes. But I
didn't go through all those different
stages, denial and anger and all that,
not at all. I did get sad, and a jolt
of fear over eternity, the inevitability, the irrevocability of death, shot
through me. Then I felt melancholy when
I realized I wouldn't do a lot of
things I wanted to. All my accomplish-
ments would be very little in this
world, and that was just the way it
would be. The well of regret filled up,
and then I had to let it drain all out.
I felt especially sad because I
wouldn't be able to see you graduate
college or get married, and I wouldn't
be able to play with your kids. That
was rough.
  At the time I couldn't find the word
for the way I felt. But then it came to
me: I felt <u>rueful</u>. I'm not sure exactly
what "rue" is, but if the feeling is
sad and sweet and sorrowful, sad regret

mixed with resignation and acceptance, then I was full of rue.

But I'm not alone when it comes to death. Mozart and Napoleon and Jack London and Madame Curie, everyone comes to the same, very democratic point. We all come to our ends, and I felt part of a great club, the only one that would accept Groucho Marx, you know? And I was relieved and unburdened, and I looked at the leaves flickering in the sun and the spider webs in the back yard and even the delirious glow on the TV, and I was happy, digging everything I could feel, tasting all the radiance, seeing all the undulating harmonics. I never understood delight, the sheer pleasure of sensation, until I was called upon to die.

And all my petty ambitions and all the things that would get me upset in the very recent past would seem too trivial and so charmingly irrelevant, and I became sweet and patient and calm. I stopped yelling at you coming home late from parties, and if there was any benefit of the doubt, I took it. I know you hoodwinked me several times, but I don't care. Love is easier than anger, and it gets better results, and I practiced loving-kindness and forgiveness and empathy like an old monk. I was leaving the world soon enough, and I skated through the little life left to me like a Buddha on ice.

Then the lab results came back and I didn't have bladder cancer or liver or pancreatic, just a small kidney stone, and I was given a new lease on life. I was happy, really, for now I would be able to enjoy the beautiful world some more. But no matter how I tried I couldn't maintain that beatific attitude. I clung to that serene spirit as best I could, but bit by bit I found myself falling back into my petty attachments, my dreary ambitions, my generalized irritability, my ego. Soon I could barely recollect my ecstatic calmness, and I returned to the world of half-baked distractions, I resumed my ego's roller-coaster rides of the daily brain, and I would get pissed off at you and all the typical crap of life.

I regretted not dying.

If I had my choice, I would have died younger and more often.

Adieu

How the brain can eat a piece of candy
only to spit it out years later,
an absurd, undigested bonbon.

HILTON OBENZINGER

Theology

"It's as I've often said," Luther told his wife. "I'm like a ripe shit and the world is like a gigantic asshole."

He knew it was the Devil who would not let him shit, the Devil would not let the turd that was Martin Luther pass through this world, and he sat for days praying in his privy.

Salvation by faith is the doctrine of a man who wants to shit but who cannot, Luther concluded. My will to shit is of no avail, and I must sit anxiously, perspiring, hoping, and praying that my shit will come like grace itself, a sweeter message hidden in the stink, an unpredictable, miraculous breakthrough.

Finally, after four or five days, his guts undulated, his sphincter took hold, and his Shit-Soul slid out.

Shitting is such a consummate pleasure, he thought, because at one certain, special moment, free will and necessity are combined.

"I was born again," he told his wife when he was done. "I entered paradise itself through open gates."

SEVEN

Family Meal

When the elder Blair died, the family gathered—three sons and a daughter with their children—and they ate Grandpa.

Some anthropologists tell of certain tribes in the South Pacific who eat their relatives when they die as a way of keeping their loved one's presence and power inside them. The spirit is absorbed, while the dross is ejected as shit. The anthropologists call such practices "affectionate cannibalism."

So the Blairs solemnly sat around the darkened dinner table, candles burning, and each chewed their morsel of roasted Grandpa.

"No, we're not Jeffrey Dahmers," Jonathan Blair explained to me afterwards, referring to the deranged serial murderer. "Remember, he *killed* his homosexual sex partners. The shrinks say he never wanted them to leave, so in his madness he murdered them and ate them instead. Of course, we didn't kill Grandpa—and we know he is gone, and we know we're not perverts. We're eating him for love, just as he ate his own father. That's the way it is with our family: 'The son shall devour the father.' Nowadays we don't limit it just to the sons or to the fathers, of course."

Very feminist, I thought.

"How did such a family tradition come to be?"

Jonathan Blair sat me down and told me the strange tale of the shipwreck of his great-great-great grandfather, a captain of a merchantman, and his son, his first mate, which I will now relate to you.

Failure

Of course, why hadn't I thought of it before? *Failure Associates!*

When the bridge collapses, when the nuclear power plant melts down, when the airplane drops out of the sky, they send out their engineers to figure out why. They calibrate the tensile strength or crank the gizmo that went bonkers or calculate the chemical reaction of spit which made the car battery explode—whatever. They gave me a tour of their labs—at that time they had a whole room filled with water heaters, dozens and dozens of them, and guys in white coats blowing them up one by one. It was impressive, all those bright white water heaters lined up, ready to explode for science and commerce.

Failure is their special niche—and how could they go wrong? You just can't lose with failure. There's always going to be failure, that's all there is to it, it's one of those laws of nature, and I would always have plenty of work, an endless parade of flops and catastrophes. I knew I had finally found my place, my home.

But I had to convince them first. They said they didn't think they had any use for a writer, but I argued plenty hard: "What about failures of nerve, failures of the heart, failures of the soul, the whole kit and caboodle? Just think of what a writer could do to expand your business! Besides, those engineers can't write worth a damn and someone needs to draw up the reports. Am I right?"

Structural Failure
Human Failure
Words Fail Me
FEETS DON'T FAIL ME NOW!

HILTON OBENZINGER

Our Lady of Shit

So it's a mission, a calling, like making people pray or laugh, I don't see any difference because it happened I took a crap one day and when I heard the ripe turd splash into the toilet, it was like a light bulb you know went off and for most people flushing the toilet is a kind of muted spiritual thing, getting rid of the unholy in one sucking gulp, and you read a book or a magazine on the toilet just to make sure you remember the difference between your head and your ass, yet I thought it was a trick, one of those tricks God puts right in your face but you're liable to miss it because you flush it away, so look at the Bible and see if I'm right: you never see Jesus shit or Mary shit because if they did there would be little bags of shit in churches, holy relics everywhere, and since the Book never says that the absence of shit makes shit even more special, if you can only open your wisdom eye and see the secret which is simple: "God is Shit and Shit is God." Then when I read that Gandhi would clean the chamber pots of one of his disciples every day I knew he knew and I realized that was my mission, to clean the toilets of God, and every day I make my rounds to restaurants and stores and gas stations and Macy's and Bloomingdale's and any public toilet with bowl brush and paper towels and 409 hanging from the special outfit I rigged inside the big yellow raincoat to be inconspicuous and I wipe the seat and I scrub the bowl I can't do much with the floor and sometimes they can be hopelessly messy especially with men peeing all over the place on the ceiling on the walls so I concentrate on the bowl and the seat, it's an endless task since people are always shitting and it's not as if I expect to finish, I have my whole life and even my next one, but I know at least plenty of janitors thank me and even those wealthy shoppers who relieve themselves and ho hum expect a clean commode is a clean commode and all of the universe exists just to wipe their delicate rectums clean driving their fat SUVs and you know even

*though they might be idiots and spoiled and thoughtless but the
fact is they're the beautiful turds of God too, and they're right
because the universe really does exist just to flush away their holy
shit*

Such considerations are perhaps of small comfort today,
since these sorts of things either matter or they don't,
according to what we're looking for.

Detective

Located Tania. In northern B.C. growing pot. Married a
Vietnam vet. He's got an interesting story: from a
Philadelphia Mainline family, he's gung-ho, doesn't even
wait for the draft, signs up for Nam, gets plenty combat, in
fact becomes expert killer, but then he's blown apart and
when he's glued back together, kind of an Ahab patch job,
he comes back home to realize Evil of the war, radicalized,
goes crazy like Ahab too, so off he goes, blows up draft
boards across the country like they were a string of white
whales, and when the war ends we find our man a fugitive,
deep underground. After Patty gets nabbed he hooks up
with Tania when his own aboveground support network
takes her on, so they travel together as a couple, soon
becoming one, and when the Feds scramble the Puerto
Rican *independistas* and after a remnant of the Weather
people botch the Brinks robbery in '81, the underground
unravels, the heat is impossible, so they make their way to
B.C. and settle down to low-key cultivation under assumed

names. People figure they lay low like others in the pot trade, so there's nothing conspicuous about the two.

I find out her whereabouts from ex-SDS Vancouver street freak who peddles nickel bags to keep skin and bone, so he knows who his connection is, naturally. But I move in slow, not wanting her to get skittish and dive back underground. I hang out in the nearby trading post looking for work, find a shack, make myself known, bide my time, until one day I visit their cabin and I pop it:

"Patty is looking for you, she wants to see you."

"Patty? Who—what are you talking about?"

"Don't need to bullshit me, Tania, I know it's you, and I'm no agent or cop of any sort, just a private party, so to speak, sent to find you for private purposes. I help people recover their past lives, and Patty Hearst wants to talk."

Her old man swings out a .38, and points it at me, which I figured he would.

"Hey, you don't need a murder rap to rattle the good cover you got here."

"What do you want?" he barks at me.

"Like I told Tania, Patty wants to see her, wants to find out what happened after they went their separate ways. Curiosity, I suppose. Maybe regrets. I'm not sure."

"What kind of nostalgia bullshit is this?" she shoots back.

"Should I *off* this pig?" her partner asks at the same moment, his finger itchy on the trigger.

"Exactly—just typical nostalgia bullshit," I try to calm him down. "No big deal."

"What's with Patty Hearst?" she eyes me. "Isn't John Waters enough?"

That's the signal I was waiting for, so I smile and say, "John Waters is the movies. This is real life."

While Constipation results from jolts of Fear,

Abject Terror ends in Diarrhea.

Manuscript

He hadn't seen him for years, and the Mojave had gotten pretty thin, though he still seemed stocky, stump-like.

"Well, lookee here," he said, extending his hand as the Indian came through the door. "Where you been hiding, Jack?"

He offered Jack some tea, avoiding even the hint of beer. The many times he had to extract Jack from bars, and Jack had forced beers on the white guy just to get him to join him in a bit of half-jovial, half-violent complicity, had not escaped him.

"I'm living on skid row now, you know, 6th Street."

"Oh, that's too bad," he exclaimed. He hoped he would be lucky and the encounter would only end up with him getting hit up for a twenty-dollar bill.

"Naw, skid row's just another kind of Rez, don't you know? It's great. I hang out with the Skins at the public library"—he inwardly flinched at the idea that Jack was reduced to the gang who sucked on their brown bags on the lawn in the shadow of the neoclassical behemoth at the Civic Center—"and it's better than you think. In fact, I started writing. Wrote up some stories about skidrow, and I want to know what you think of them, if you think they could be published."

Out came a slim manuscript, and the price for the encounter had changed from some panhandling to free editorial consultation, maybe even a little of both, though he was not much relieved. He expected the writing to be awful, and he geared up for careful skirting of the truth.

He skimmed the top story, a little sketch about white women wanting to hit up on Indian men, some kind of lust-for-the-savage crap, which the skidrow Skins played up to the hilt for pussy. The writing was much better than he had expected, but it all seemed so strange. They had been like brothers once, as they worked to free Jack from the attempted bombing charge that was entangled with Arizona Mafia and big-money developer types and Feds, all attempting to lay the rap on the Injun to keep their own dirty deals buried, even though I had little doubt that Jack may have shoved a stick or two of dynamite under the BIA for his own good reasons. Booze and white pussy didn't seem to be what everything would add up to after the charges were finally dropped.

Mezuzah

Hollywood, Florida, bears no relation to its California namesake, except perhaps for the fact that both cultivate illusions, though of different sorts. I would walk with my still-vigorous ninety-year-old father along the misnamed concrete boardwalk, the crystal waves of the Atlantic glittering, and I would observe the crowds marching back and forth on their respective constitutionals. Elderly Jews from New York or thereabouts would chug and limp and shuffle to keep the juices flowing for the sake of life itself, all the while chatting in Yiddish or Yiddish-inflected English. Passing like ships in the night were middle-aged Quebecois vacationers on holiday chattering in their clipped, North American French. They politely shared the turf, hardly exchanging glances, each group comfortably encamped on its own happy, linguistic island, oblivious to the other, though how both the French Canadians and the New York Jews had come to stake out the very same beach remained a mystery.

But there arose a more immediate mystery to solve. At the very end of the boardwalk, when the pavement met the wooden fence of private property, someone had put up a good-sized mezuzah, the Jewish amulet stuffed with a verse from the Book ordinarily nailed to a doorpost. The elderly Jews spry enough to reach the end of the boardwalk (about two miles) would kiss their hand and pat the little, wooden box, then make their about-face and hustle back on their return lap.

Then one morning, when the very first walkers reached the fence, they were shocked to discover only the pale outline of where the mezuzah used to hang. Someone had pried the sucker off the wall.

All Jewish eyes turned suspiciously toward Quebec.

Satan's Asshole

Rhea Perlman and Danny DeVito observed the police car drive back down their driveway in stunned silence.

Rhea was the first to find her voice.

"Why didn't you tell them?" she asked.

"Are you kidding?" Danny softly responded. "I should tell them that some guy pointed an Uzi at my head, yapped about Dante, and then suddenly disappeared? Should I tell them that he was sucked underground just like . . . *poof?*"

Confused, they both stared at the ground, Danny stamping his foot delicately on the not-so terra firma.

"They'd think I was crazy, and when the tabloids got hold of it—jeez," he sighed.

"What're we going to do, Danny?"

Father

I had never felt so awkward in my life, sitting before this young man who looked exactly like me. "Spitting image," they like to say, and I did feel almost like spitting at him. Maybe I could muss up his unnerving exactitude with a little bodily fluid. But my bodily fluids had already messed him up enough, so I just sat there in the hotel lobby, rubbing my palms on my knees and smiling unrelentingly like someone on speed. I couldn't speak.

"I know this is a little strange," he started up, "but you don't have to do anything. You don't even need to say anything."

I smiled, staring, speechless.

"I always wanted to find my father. But I never expected to look exactly like him."

I shrugged, nodded, kept smiling.

"My mother never told me much about you. I don't think she really knew, anyway."

I stared.

"You know I'm a Christian minister, don't you?"

I nodded again, trying to decide when to tell him his father is Jewish.

"In my church we pray for the spirit to descend, the Holy Spirit, and we aren't surprised when the holiness does come upon us. It could happen at any time." He paused, his glance drooping to my left shoulder. "Well, I believe there is some Divine plan in our meeting, a way that the Holy Spirit is speaking to us or through us."

"And what does the spirit say?" I blurted out.

Through rectums all Emotions are expressed,
Thus Souls with farts through sphincters must eject.

Mezuzah

My mother stared out the pane glass window of the twenty-sixth floor, the Atlantic to the right, the Intercoastal waterway to the left, condos and lush greenery all around, and in the distance Ft. Lauderdale rising up like white acne on the horizon. It was a stunning view, but all she did now was to stare, sometimes counting the cars as they whizzed by South Ocean Drive, a kind of pointless game, hardly saying a word. I knelt by her side, trying to imagine what went on inside an eighty-six-year-old brain that I thought I had known so intimately but was now so alien, so insular, drifting in dementia.

I could see police cars with flashing lights careening down South Ocean Drive. Heading for the boardwalk, I speculated. The "Mezuzah War" was in full swing, and some Jewish geezer might have pushed a Quebecois on the paddle ball court, or a Kanuck might have stuck his foot out as he sat on the benches by the band shell and tripped some strolling Yid. It was a pathetic conflict, nothing like the intensity of the Middle East, but ever since the mezuzah had disappeared from its usual perch at the end of the boardwalk, the beach was polarized. The Cubans tended to side with the Jews, while the Haitians sympathized with their fellow Francophones, though neither group chose to set foot in the war zone, preferring instead to watch the hostilities from afar.

Then all the brouhaha after the Bush-Gore election boiled over, the scandal over botched votes and pregnant chads just before the great horror of September 11th.

"If you like counting cars so much, why not go to Ft. Lauderdale and count votes," I joshed her, as she regarded her accustomed view from the twenty-sixth floor.

She smiled at the small joke—I was gratified she had at least a slight grip on current events—and, as she let out a ripple of soft laughs, the fist she had held tightly in her lap rolled open.

To my amazement, the missing wooden mezuzah rested gently in the palm of her hand.

Manuscript

In one of Jack's stories a little baby shows up outside the door of their ratty studio on 6th Street.

"A baby? Is this true?"

"Yeah, some bitch, I don't know who, just dropped it off, a little girl, with a note saying she was ours. One of us Skins must be the father, at least we figure. We can't tell who, but she looks like one or all of us, so we're raising her up ourselves all together."

The Indian seemed unaware of the strangeness of such an arrangement.

"On skid row?"

"No problem," he assured me. "Skid row's just another kind of Rez."

Family Meal

When they picked up young Blair from the lifeboat, he was alone, the sole survivor of the shipwreck.

He said nothing of his ordeal until, months later, on August 21, 1819, he sailed into Boston harbor. Then, after his mother's tearful welcome home was spent, a joy for his return amply mixed with grief over the loss of her husband, he told her the truth of what had transpired in the lifeboat: his father's secret sacrifice.

At first she shuddered at the horror of the dying father having asked the son to batten upon his corpse so that the boy may subsist the many weeks adrift. Other sailors had been forced to cannibalism, horrible as that may be, but no chronicles told of a son feasting on his own father. How could the senior Blair have even contemplated such a hideous gift? And then she wept at how tender her good husband was, even at the end, and how brave he had been to offer himself so that his only son should live.

"Here," the survivor said, holding a small package, some worn canvas folded and tied with a string. "We have nothing to bury, unless I should be the one who is interred, now that father lives on in my flesh. But long after the horrid, mournful meal, when I finally did relieve myself, I gathered as best as I could the evidence of my bowels to bring home. Now we can at least attend to my father's grave."

Head bowed, he offered his mother the little package of dung.

EIGHT

Mars Virus

She had been living in her shack in Humboldt County so long she had forgotten just how intelligent walls could be. Now she was standing in the tube of the airport terminal gently feeling along the wall, delighted at its undulations but also scared. She could hardly imagine the ancient lumber of her shack vibrating with nanodigital sensors— the idea was laughable. But now she would have to accustom herself once again to the softly pliant, yet firmly vibrant intelligence of surfaces.

Suddenly, she fell forward. The tube had begun to close in on her, contracting and expanding repeatedly, then effortlessly writhing, pushing her ahead like she was a mouse stuck in a snake's gullet. The corridor had determined her hesitation to be of no logical necessity, so she found herself swiftly squeezed along in its intestinal, peristaltic motions. It was soon time for her to be dumped, and at the tube's sphincter-like end she was deposited in the waiting room before the grinning face of the ticket-counter monitor.

"Window or aisle seat?" the face on the video wall inquired.

Selection

Some people are almost transparent. Their bones, organs, and the rest swim in a thick yet virtually invisible jelly. Other people are opaque, and all you can see is a pasty glow of light shining through them. A few rare cases, however, are invisible, to be located simply by the thin dark smudge forming their outlines. Only novices desire the transparent jelly or opaque types, and they are usually left to wither. Real aficionados find it far more sporting to stalk the invisible ones, since all you have to go on is a thin, greasy blur, and all your instincts are called into play just to find them, much less fuck them.

Plan

"Kill your father and marry your mother."

"Oh, come on, now, you can do better than that. How about you kill your mother and marry your father?"

"Hmm. Not bad. Why don't you simply kill your mother *and* your father and just masturbate over their dead bodies?"

"Better yet, you sleep with your mother *and* your father, and then kill yourself."

"That's a plan. Or you could sleep with your daughter and kill your mother."

"Lovely, but incomplete. Better that I sleep with my daughter *and* my mother, then kill my father."

"And then kill yourself."

"*Absolutely.*"

"I think we have a plan."

There is such a gap between the ideal and the grossly actual
that I may say I am as yet unborn.

Our Lady of Shit

Sometimes Our Lady of Shit Mother Theresa of the Toilets or Saint Tidybowl or Holy Shit or simply The Shit Lady—I have become a crackpot an eccentric female Emperor Norton wandering San Francisco with a mop, someone's barroom anecdote type thing, and that's OK just fine, they know the calling, they see what has to be done and they wonder why does someone clean the shit, and they can wonder at the landfills the barges of sludge the cyclones of bottles and tin cans it's all the same sweet spring as Calistoga Water the same huge Pacific Ocean. Sometimes I find things left behind in the toilets, shit in the can so to speak, coins and girlie magazines oozing condoms half eaten apples candy bars even love letters even a suicide note once and even a suicide himself hugging the bowl in a pool of blood. But one day I found a silvery rectangle and the box was filled with slides and when I held them up to the light I was astonished to discover they were pictures of me and my parents and my brother and even the photo with Danny DeVito when he came back home to New Jersey and a shiver went up my spine. Why was it left why was the tin can of pictures left behind who had the photos of my past and what about the captions, did they steal the captions the explanations of vacations and events, why did they take them why leave them why have them in the first place? I was perplexed but not surprised really. Some Body was leaving messages as if all my life was waiting for me, and I had one of those epiphanies, one of those God Fucks, namely that these slides were all just another pile of turds, and God had dropped the shit of my family history right here in the crapper in Macys just like God had dropped the suicide in Starbucks SO I COULD CLEAN HIM UP, so I could prove memory has its own 409 its own Lysol, so I wiped the box clean and I put it under my coat and took it home.

Be all you can be

To be or not to be

Don't worry, be happy

The First Human Be-In

Just be your self

Whatever will be, will be

The be-all end-all

Be that as it may

Let It Be

Knowing

I stood in his apartment with the police, saw the refrigerator and freezer where the gore was preserved, leaned against the kitchen counter where I would learn afterwards he had carved the flesh off of the bones of his victims, and it all seemed so ordinary. Only later would the full horror sink in.

I knew from his previous molestation charges that my son could only love other men or boys. But that was hardly the worst of it. He was filled with a terrible, unutterable emptiness, and he could only love the men he would meet if they couldn't move, if the object of his love was still and kept quiet, and he could control him. So he would wait in the bushes with a baseball bat for the jogger of his desire and knock him out. Death would be the ultimate control, of course, and the dead in their hushed stillness would in the end become the primary objects of his sexual appetite.

He dreaded abandonment, was terrified of people running away from him, leaving him, maybe because of my divorce from his mother or when, in her own madness, his mother moved out of the house and simply left him behind. So he yearned to control his victims, and he would meet men in the bathhouses and drug them, then put his ear to their abdomen and listen to their heart and organs, reduce their whole being, their individual identities, to mere parts and bodily functions. He wanted to fix them in his grasp, to make them a part of him so they would never leave, and he even drilled holes in a few of their skulls while they were drugged and poured acid in their brains as an experiment to see if he could create a lobotomized zombie, someone he could utterly control. He failed, and his victims always died, although one stayed alive for two days, and I cannot imagine that man's unspeakable pain and horror.

But even though he had sex with his dead partners, he could not allay his fear of abandonment. The body would rot, eventually sounds would no longer come from its stomach, it could not stay; even the dead, stinking and putrid, would abandon him. Another still, dead body would have to take its place. I am sure the only reason he began to eat his victims was to make them a permanent part of him. Cannibalism was just another way to ensure that they would never leave him, that they would be a part of him forever, although that didn't work either. Once in the stomach they were there, sure enough, but they were also gone.

But cannibalism wasn't the worst of it. Far worse was the realization that my son was only the deeper, darker shadow of his father. I am not a homosexual, but I had the same dread, the same suffocating shyness, the same fear that I would be abandoned when I was young. I would wake up in the middle of the night with the unnerving sense that I had murdered someone, even though it was only a dream. I never did cross the line from dream to hideous perversity the way my son did—I would toy with ants and set them on fire but I never imagined toying with the life of a man. Yet that was of little comfort. After months of holding it in, of repressing the thought, I realized that I really did know the true source of my own son's deadly lunacy. It was me.

After the session, you get to choose your new ego.

Bet

So the three of them, two Hoopas and a Yurok, were on the bridge over the Klamath at Martin's Ferry, a high steel bridge veering off the one-lane blacktop that heads fifteen or twenty miles down to the dead end at Johnson's, the bridge connecting with the dirt road making its way maybe twenty-four miles to Orrick on the coast, kind of too much of a bridge for such feeble roads, big sturdy steel beams like the Bay bridge, but the bridge was so high, I dunno, maybe sixty, maybe one-hundred feet, and was so isolated, a car crossing every hour, sometimes less, that it got to be popular with the white people who would come to the reservation, drive to the bridge, tie their lines and bungee jump.

Really?

Boing boing like a rubber band above the river, and since hardly anyone was there—maybe an Indian would come by, but why would he concern himself with a foolish white man bouncing on a rubber band?—the jumpers never got bothered, and it was a regular sight to see strange *waugai* throw themselves off the bridge and snap back up, kind of crazy but thrilling, too.

What about the three guys?

I'm getting to that. So the three of them were on the Martin Ferry's bridge drunk and horsing around when one of the Hoopas dares the Yurok: "I'll bet you a hundred dollars you can't bungee jump off the bridge without a bungee cord."

What?

Bungee jump off the bridge without a bungee cord.

That's insane. How can you bungee jump without a bungee cord, you're just jumping off the bridge period, that's all.

Only if you think so, it's just another way of looking at it. In any case, they taunt each other and yell and finally the guy says OK, climbs up on the railing, and in a second he pushes himself off. The two other guys run to the edge to see him drop into the water—no *boing boing* of course but it was spring and the river was still pretty deep—and for the longest time that was the last they saw of him until downstream his head bobs up and drifts down to a gravel bar and he pulls himself out of the river unhurt or at least he didn't feel anything, although later they found he did crack a couple of ribs, so he climbs back up to the road and to the bridge where the other two are hooting and hollering, laughing that he actually took the dare, and he just walks up to them almost sober now and grabs a beer and says, "Pay up—you owe me a hundred bucks."

When you eat the poisonous root "sardaine"

you die

with a hideous laugh-like grimace

frozen on your face.

Hence the origin of the word "sardonic."

Religion

The Mothers and Fathers of God have a very simple concept, an idea so obvious it is a mystery why it took until the end of the twentieth century for people to discover true religion.

Rather than the usual God-the-Father, Oliver Menard, the Grand Parent, proclaimed that the truth was just the reverse: the Deity is God-the-Child, and we humans are merely reluctant Foster Parents.

All of the Deity's cruelty and jealousy and petulance can be explained in an instant. The creation of the universe was mere child's play, his toying with humans just a game. God may have created everything, but He was still a kid, and humanity has been forced to become Foster Parents to protect His creation from His thoughtless mischief.

"We have a terrible responsibility," as the Grand Parent would say. "We must guide God with Tough Love."

Oliver Menard explained how humans had to have the highest moral standards, so that God would follow our example. And we had to point out His failings unflinchingly or all the many creatures of planets known and unknown would have to suffer His petulance and irrational violence forever.

When the Jews celebrate Passover, we go into mourning for the Egyptian soldiers who were so blithely drowned in the Red Sea.

Once a year we observe Cain's Day, mourning the time God smacked His lips over Abel's offering of sizzling steak, but frowned upon Cain's gift of couscous. Cain's Day is a vegetarian feast day to honor God's victim during which we bemoan why He chose one parent above the other. The birth of murder was not Cain's fault, but caused by God toying with favors from his parents. Cain's Day feasts are always filled with cautionary tales, warning us to avoid the Big Child's manipulations.

During Ramadan we fast all night as well as all day. Foster Parents strong enough hold a month-long hunger strike to protest the Kid's temper tantrums.

At Easter, Christians sing praises for the resurrection of who they think is the "Son" of God without realizing that Jesus was actually an exemplary Foster Parent. "Father, why hast thou forsaken me" is reported incorrectly in the Gospels. God said this to Jesus, and not the other way around. During this time we weep for Mary as the Mother of God, while we celebrate her for being the mother of Jesus, who was God's Perfect Yet Abused Father.

Oliver Menard ordained a very strict moral code, since humanity's job was to educate the Spoiled Infant, and while there has been some progress, and God has tried to budget his Moral Expense Account somewhat more responsibly, we still have a long, long way to go.

The Mothers and Fathers of God even has an eschatological prophecy. No apocalyptic cataclysm, no sudden bang, and no thousand years of the Grand Parent's rule. Instead, a slow maturing of the Deity parallels His Parents' own descent into old age, a kind of cosmic crisscrossing of generations—the boomers die out while the Kid itches for their social security. Scholars estimate that God is currently in the middle of adolescence. At least the Deity is no longer teething, as He was during Noah's time, but you can see just how dangerous the situation has become. God is a teenage delinquent!

Eventually, humans will become feeble, used up, and God will put us in The Dark Nursing Home, no matter how loudly we protest. But the question remains: Will He have matured enough to guide the universe wisely? Will humans be allowed the comfort of at least knowing that we tamed the Brat before we fade away?

All my life I have been dying of laughter.

Perfect Peace

There is no perfect peace in individuality. You cannot stand still. That is why I pray for peace, for motionlessness. I want to feel like some plant, ingesting life without seeking it, existing without individual sensation. So I sit in my chair, very still, and I absorb life with no "Me," with no feeling separating me from the ones I love, just the still, quiet peacefulness of plants. This makes me happy.

If you cannot accept ego loss,
you may complain of strange bodily symptoms.

Two Mothers

They had arrived at the village just as the funeral procession snaked its way to the cemetery. They recognized her, the gray-haired Jewish American woman who truly understood their agony of living under Israeli rule, and they embraced her as a grandmother, a friend, and a comrade. She stepped from the car, and they pushed her to the head of the crowd, wailing and shouting *Allah ul akhbar* in grief and rage and pride, several of the young men carrying the bier with the dead teenager wrapped in his white shroud and covered with the Palestinian flag. Another martyr of the *Al Aksa Intifida*, another boy shot in the head by an Israeli soldier, of almost the same age, another hero of the liberation struggle to be buried, and as always the funeral became a complicated ritual of catharsis that broke down all differences and degrees, a theater in which they were all the actors and none spectators. Their Jewish guest was astonished by the power of the procession, the sense that the human mass was itself a living creature lifting her off her feet and forward, no matter what her will.

They came to the freshly dug grave, the crowd pushing to the edge of the pit. There, in the upturned soil at the bottom, rested the bones of another son, one who had died years earlier in the first *Intifada*, the bones long before cleaned of all flesh, and in an instant the wailing mother leaped into the grave, grabbed the skull and femurs and began kissing the bones in a passion of grief and love, a mother ready to sacrifice yet another child to the soil of her homeland, her children becoming the soil itself.

The American tried to push back away from the awful scene, but the crowd, its hysteria reaching an almost unbearable pitch, kept pushing her forward. She felt dizzy, alarmed by the excess of emotion, horrified at the ghastly sight of the mother kissing the bones of her son. She tried to get a grip on herself, to dig her heels into the ground, but the crowd kept surging and shoving forward, wailing and shouting, until finally she could no longer hold on. The dirt on the edge of the grave gave way, her feet slid downwards. Clawing at the shrieking women beside her, she tumbled into the hole, falling headfirst onto the skull and its mother.

NINE

Book of Jonah

The real reason I don't want to go to Nineveh to argue with the people there is precisely because I know they would believe me. No doubt I would convince them, they would repent, and God would hold off having the earth swallow them up.

That's the problem. Once again I would be laughed at and scorned as a liar or a mere novelist because the worst thing that could possibly happen did not. They'll end up happy and successful and living good, unremarkable lives—treating me like a fraud.

It would be better for my reputation if some insignificant town would truly get demolished. Then I would have some real standing and no one would dare give me even the smallest smirk. Probably the next town I summoned to repent after a good sinkhole would do just that, shivering in their socks, then the next, and the next—until, after a dozen or so towns, the cataclysm would fade, recede into memory, and the murderous consequences of inattentiveness would become nothing but a vague rumor. Sure enough, no one believes me when I say they would get sucked into hell if they don't change their ways. They *do* end up changing their ways, of course, but only because of the strength of my arguments, not because they believe my threats. I want fear, and all I get is reason—can you imagine that?—and it isn't worth it.

So I quit.

This accounts for why I am still in the bowels of this whale. Resignation not accepted. And no apology seems enough for God, so I have spent years in the darkness of this creature, listening to his huge heart rushing in and out like Manhattan traffic, watching plankton and weeds and whole Titanics suck into his gut.

There's plenty of action and hardly a quiet moment, but I still have time enough to think, to mull over the great questions of life. The whale swallowed an Office Depot truck months ago (how its driver took a dive into the deep blue sea remains a mystery), and I fished out reams of paper and pens, even a desk and a chair, before the wreck headed out of the creature's rear end. I have set myself up in a corner of his stomach to write. If the public wants to scoff at me as a mere novelist, I'll do their bidding; I will write the story of how a handsome prince was swept from the muddy margins of life and sent on a journey to the center of the earth in search of . . .

Well, now you must read my tale—or else the entire world will perish!

Bet

At first the guy who bet him backed off, said he never really meant it, didn't think anyone would be so crazy as to actually take him up on it and jump off the bridge without a bungee cord, said the fact that you're still breathing is payoff enough, all that kind of talk, but the jumper kept on insisting that he fork up his hundred-dollar wager. Finally they began to fight, slugging and pounding each other until they both knocked each other's lights out, and they woke up the next morning stretched out on the bridge, sore and hungover, but glad.

"Do you think I'm kidding or something, *motherfucker*?"

Kwame's Nightmare

Kwame found himself in a revolving door in front of Macy's. How he got there he didn't know, only that he was circling around and around and he couldn't get out. He yelled for someone to stop the whirligig, to jam the doors, but nobody seemed to hear him, and when the door whirled to the opening in front or to the one behind, the gap snapped by too quickly for him to leap out. He was startled to see a woman in a yellow slicker suddenly running alongside him in the small space. Why was she there? Could she help? He tried to ask, but no words came out. Then the woman lifted her arms and she had toilet bowl brushes instead of hands, and huge fingernails sprung out like knives from the toilet bowl brushes. She lunged at him, tearing at his face, his arms, his chest—the blood splattering the glass. And still the revolving door would not stop, while his shrieks circled around and around with his gore.

No End in Sight

Modern Thoreau

I live in Palo Alto—a renter, mere condo trash—and people here advise me not to fork over my spare change to the homeless, panhandling on the sidewalks. I will only encourage them, they argue. They will not clean themselves; they will persist in booze; they will not work. Most of all, what little I give them will confirm the opinion of all beggars that our town is filled with easy marks. The homeless scum will thus flock to our clean, prosperous streets to harvest our coins, and their presence will lower the "quality" of our lives.

In fact, this prospect appeals to me, and I readily hand out my quarters and dimes precisely because I want to encourage the congregation of the homeless. The unclean vagrant is probably more comfortable in his skin than the hygienic miser, and I know that a man who desperately needs a drink deserves one, unless he decides on his own to climb aboard the wagon. Besides, I salute all who choose not to work, if indeed the choice is theirs, and I seek to support them in their noble decision. And if labor has been taken from them, if they have been tossed aside, discarded by those who say they do not need them and who then condemn them for being not needed, then to stand on the sidewalk as an object of scorn is labor enough, and all who pass by are obliged to pay their wages

But most of all, I give to the homeless because I want to irritate the rich. If more homeless flock to these streets, I can only be glad that the smug, complacent jackasses who ignore them should feel "put upon."

The End Justifies The Means

Dear Boy,
  Andy's working valet parking at the Sheraton in Palo Alto when a truck driver pulls up right in front to make a delivery and Andy tells him he's got

to move, seeing as he's right in front of the hotel where they pick up the cars, but the driver won't move, won't listen to reason. They yell, then they start slugging it out, and in no time Andy gets the shit kicked out of him. Management calls the cops, but neither one of them wants to get the law involved, so they don't press charges, and Andy's boss tells him to go home for the day. The trucker—an immigrant from Nigeria known as a tough customer—moves to the back, but only after telling Andy he would kill him if he got in the trucker's way again. "You don't know who you're messing with," Andy retorts, and he's right, the trucker didn't realize that he was playing right into Andy's paranoid delusions. Here at last was someone who was really out to get him.

So Andy goes to his car, pulls out the piece he keeps in his glove compartment, and as the trucker stands looking over his map to locate his next stop, Andy walks up to him and shoots him in the back of his head.

Just like that.

Filipino Gulf War vet, shattered, lost, lover dead from AIDS, paranoid, afraid of the world, attacked from all sides—now your cousin is facing the death penalty, and it's all so crazy.

People mourn the dead man, and they should—five kids, sending all his money back home to Nigeria—but they think of Andy as some vicious animal or worse, though he's only a lost soul, and when his parents visit him in jail he tells them he feels safer inside than out in the world. So he's finally found a way to put himself in a box. The cops like to make him into a "bad guy," and the dead man is the "good guy," but it's rarely so simple. Andy did wrong, killed a man, but lots of times there's hardly a difference between the victim and the murderer, it's only a question of which lost soul crosses the threshold first.

Adieu

To What End?

The Middle Way

He always waited for a movie to begin before taking his seat, and he would find out the film's length and set a little alarm on his wrist watch so he could leave just before it came to an end. He arrived at baseball games during the second inning, and left right after the eighth. He was never the first to come to a party and never the last to leave. He would start novels with chapter two and leave

HILTON OBENZINGER

off right before the last one. Lovemaking was the same (although he did achieve orgasm and allowed his girlfriend the same pleasure only because, enlightened as he was, he knew that climax was not the end). He would even run indoors when the sun set, and while he could stay up all night working or partying, he would never step outside to marvel at the dawn.

Some things didn't seem to have a marked beginning or end. You could find the mouth of a river and call it an end, but it's hard to find the very beginning (and he was definitely not one to join the Hindu pilgrimage to the source of the Ganges). A lake or an ocean, however, seems to have no start or finish, and he would jump into the water without trying to wade in, preferring to leap from dry to wet without any transition. No sea shore, just sea and shore, and this way he could avoid what could be understood as the place where the Pacific begins.

He avoided anything with a beginning or an ending, opting for the great middle instead, and anyone who knew him got used to his eccentricity or phobia. Those points of abrupt transition filled him with dread, no matter how gentle, like a sunrise, or meaningful, like the end of a suspense film. If someone told him how the movie would end, he was grateful, not irked, just so long as he left before the conversation itself came to an end.

Unkind acquaintances would taunt him: "What about birth? What about death?"

He was unaware of his birth, he would explain, and his death, as an ending, he was sure would kill him, which is why he avoided it.

"Life," shrugged the bombardier, "is a complicated wince."

Our Lady of Shit

Dead cells dead bacteria all of ourselves some undigested fiber sure but mostly the droppings of our own flesh, a constant, even when we are born sometimes we shit before we breathe before we eat and we shit even after we die, and when the archeologists found the first products of people they found what they call "coprolites" which means simply fossil shit ahead of all the rest, something special and even in ancient days it was special; shit used for cosmetics smeared on ladies' faces; wounds and disease cured with shit; the aristocratic lady bathing in her slave's turds, though Saint Jerome condemned the practice which shows what little wisdom found its way to the Pope. Meanwhile the Samoans assign a god to each kid when they're born and they call that kid the shit of that god like "Come here, Shit of Tongo and eat your breadfruit!" Even Jeremy Bentham thinks shit should be put to good use, so cherish the droppings of your own flesh, circulate them in a great motion back to the soil to grow the food that produces the shit and wonder if you yourself are not the droppings of a far larger rectum than dreamt of in your philosophy Horatio.

To delete is to insert.

Modern Thoreau

With the advent of cloning, I make sure to give alms to the homeless for yet another reason, one far more compelling than the typical calls of charity: *I may meet my true Self on the street one day, and I should be horrified if I were unkind to the one to whom I owe all.* "Know Thyself," the adage goes, and perhaps that pile of rags huddled in a doorway against a shopping cart is more of me than I could possibly ever imagine wanting to know. I am not concerned with any golden rule; there is no "as you would unto others" in *my* love. I fear that—now that DNA has become democratic, even trivial—I *am* those others. So I fork over my spare change for selfish reasons, for there would be no unkindness worse than denying myself.

The Bitter End

Nothing

I was driving up Clipper Street, up to Twin Peaks. It was night but not too foggy, and in the rearview mirror I could see the entire panorama of the city below.

All of a sudden everything turned black. I could see nothing but blackness through the windshield, blackness in the rearview mirror.

At first I thought I had gone blind, but then I noticed I could see the lights on the dashboard and everything inside the car without any problem. I rolled down the window. I could see my car, but beyond the tire there was only inky blackness, no streetlights, no glow from houses, nothing. I couldn't even see the road when I looked down. I found myself driving according to instinct, allowing habit to direct me, at least for a few seconds, but then I got scared. In no time I would hit someone or drive into a tree, so I pulled over to where I thought the curb might be and sat with the parking brake on, wondering what to do.

I peered through the dense miasma for a long time. I had never seen anything like this before, the blackness so deep, so complete, like the thickest motor oil you could ever imagine. Then I realized I couldn't hear anything either, no noise, no grumble of passing cars, nothing.

I must be dead.

All's Well That Ends Well

Bet

"He was a meat-and-potatoes man," his wife confided.

The sheriff sat in his starched khaki uniform at the little electric Wurlitzer, pumping out skating-rink waltzes in the narrow trailer near the river on the way to Orleans, outside of the reservation, his cap off and his ruddy bald pate shining with sweat, while his wife sat on the small couch, smiling graciously at her guests. On the shelf above him the police radio crackled out messages—a brawl, a car accident—to which the sheriff cocked one ear as he bore down on the keyboard.

"Our boy was killed in Vietnam," she called out above the din, smiling tightly, as if that were some sort of explanation for the scene.

The Blue Danube throbbed, while the radio crackled about someone jumping off the bridge at Martin's Ferry.

Mars Virus

She examined the trio of scientists in their white tunics as they lined up before her in the meadow. They looked lost, even a little scared. They must not be used to standing away from their intelligent walls and moving sidewalks, she concluded. Their own feet would have to guide them now, and this was a task they were not accustomed to, and it produced odd feelings. The tallest of the three looked especially awkward, a gawky Ichabod Crane, although he probably didn't even know who Ichabod Crane was.

"You want something from a Clean Flesh Creep?" She uttered the slur slowly, deliberately. "What could a Creep possibly give *you*?"

Ichabod blushed. "Because you are a 'Creep,' as you say, we hope to draw blood and synapses from you to fashion some kind of inoculation. We don't know if it will work, but we must try."

Suddenly a look of disbelief crossed his eyes, then panic and horror, and in an instant Ichabod Crane's right arm dropped off.

The End of Time

Our Lady of Shit

When I found the box of slides left in the toilet mysterium tremendum *all the pictures of my family, I found my discarded self my family all droppings of dead memories gone and I wept over banal home scene snapshots, fingered the lost times wept again baffled at why of all things I found the collection of slides in the Macy's Lady's Room—who could have left it there? But I have no holy calling to collect shit or memories only to clean it up, to allow the circulation of bodies to keep the small wonders juggling like stars in the Milky Way. So in a few days I brought the box of slides to the Lady's Room in Grace Cathedral and I said a small prayer "Give me Liberty or Give me Birth" and left it there for the grace of God's shit to circulate the story one more time.*

Even Theology must always be a Theological warning against Theology.

Science

Heart rate increases, levels of epinephrine and norepi-nephrine rise, blood pressure rises, galvanic skin response changes—the same as fear or rage or aggression—but then you come to a fork in the road. You could pull the gun out of the glove compartment, you could flee, carried away in a torrent of adrenaline, or the chemical system could head in an entirely different direction. The blood pressure suddenly drops; tolerance to pain increases; endorphins flood the sys-tem; "fight or flight" mechanisms quickly shut down; arous-al fans out, pleasurable release flows throughout your body with no apparent "telos;" new neuronal maps burn into your brain; your jaw opens; your head tilts back; and deep guttural hoots ratchet up your gullet—*HA! HA! HA!*

The End

Wandering

Some people describe how on certain occasions their soul or consciousness suddenly leaves their body and soars off to some place far away, their flesh left idle back where they parked it until they pop back into their skin. They call this "astral projection." This phenomenon is unknown to me, but I have experienced what might be called "carnal peregrination": my soul stays put but my body wanders away on its own, inserting itself in random places.

Say I'm watching reruns of *I Love Lucy*, apparently content, when without warning my body drifts off in the middle of a gag. After a while, my consciousness, all along still in front of the TV, snaps back into my body, and suddenly I find myself in the middle of sucking down my third martini in a bar in Denver, or yelling in the bleachers during the seventh inning of a Giants game in San Francisco, or wrestling in bed with a woman I can't recognize (and once even a man!) in New York—and I have no idea how in the world I got there. My body, seemingly of its own volition and unknown to my mind, meandered over to that certain corner of the universe—how embarrassing, it's like I'm an innocent bystander—and I have to figure out how to extract my bag of bones delicately from an uncomfortable scene or out from between damp sheets and bring it back to *I Love Lucy* where it left its brains behind.

That's how I met your mother.

Knowledge is not made for understanding.
It is made for cutting.

Detective

They were shooting the last scenes of *Cecil B. Demented*, the climax. A gang of terrorists set their kidnapped movie star on fire and blow up a drive-in movie. Seems like a lot of fun. They say this is one of John Waters' campy send-ups, but I don't know—don't care, either. Patty Hearst always has some sort of role in his films, so she was playing the mother of one of the terrorists, and in this scene she drives through the explosions and chaos to rescue her son. There are all sorts of gunfire and bombs, the kid is blown off the roof of the snack stand and lands on Patty's wind-shield with a thud. Then Patty coos in a motherly fashion that her son is back. Ironic, I guess.

Well, I'm no film critic, so it didn't matter to me. What matters was that I was finally delivering Tania to my client, and not a moment too soon. She had kept her mouth shut almost the whole trip—the bus ride to Vancouver, the plane to Chicago—but once we switched planes for Baltimore she began to yak incessantly with some kind of left-wing drivel about the World Bank and globalization and such. Must have been the jitters. All of a sudden, approaching her long-lost friend, she reverted to a giant conspiracy theory of capitalist greed and stupidity. Greed-and-Stupidity is the basis of civilization, I figure, and no big surprise to me—and dumb movies likewise. But it was as if she had a nervous tic, her mouth just kept running on and on, and by the time we reached the drive-in movie lot I could barely stand another minute.

Finally, the filming came to an end. Patty got out of the car and walked towards her trailer. I caught her eye and pointed my chin at Tania without saying a word. Delight and fear crossed her face as soon as she saw her, and I could tell that Tania was likewise going through awkward, conflicted changes. They looked amazingly similar, although Patty had filled out more, her angular face somewhat rounder, the way you would expect a mother with a couple of kids to look long after her heyday.

I drifted off into the background, and Tania went up to Patty in a careful, deliberate saunter. Surrounded by actors and extras dressed like punk terrorists and motley drive-in moviegoers, all rushing back and forth in a frenzy, they stood before each other for the first time in twenty-five years.

My vision was blocked by the swarming crowd, and then a pickup with a camera on a cherry picker drove across the lot, and I couldn't even see the crowd.

By the time the pickup passed and the scene cleared, the two of them had vanished.

Dead End

Bedtime Story

"Once upon a time there was a king, and he was a good king. The people liked him, and he would pray and meditate and follow all the rules of good behavior. He was so good that one of the gods came to visit and offer him some kind of reward."

"Do you mean there was more than one god, Dad?"

"Sure, any good story has to have more than one god. We got gods to spare."

"What about devils?"

"Plenty of devils too."

The boy looked worried, and his father pulled the covers to his son's chin.

"Don't worry—there are more gods than devils."

"So what was the reward?" the little boy asked.

"Well, I was trying to tell you. The god came to the king and asked him what he wanted, said that he would grant him his wish, and the king said he wanted immortality."

"What's that?"

"He asked the god if he could live forever."

"Oh."

"In any case, the god said he couldn't grant that wish. Immortality was reserved for gods only, and no human could become a god.

"The king was disappointed. The god stroked his chin, cooking up a scheme, and finally he said, 'I can't make you immortal, but I can put conditions on the way you can die. Air-tight conditions.'

"'What do you mean?' asked the king.

"'You cannot die indoors or outdoors, and you cannot die in the daytime or the nighttime. Plus no weapon can kill you—no knives, no guns, no cannons, no arrows. What do you think?'

"The king considered what the god had offered, and he could not calculate any way to be killed in that scheme. Indoors or outdoors? Nighttime or daytime? No weapons? The king took the deal, grateful for the reward that, while not official immortality, seemed pretty much the same thing.

"Well, the king got so arrogant because he thought he would live forever that he abused the people. He raised their rents, put down heavy taxes, and went from being a good king to being a mighty bad one—executing anyone who complained, stealing their daughters to become his wives even though they would kick and scream—so many bad things—all because he thought no one could kill him. He acted with what people call 'impunity.'"

"He was puny?"

"No, impunity—acting like there were no consequences, no one holding him back."

"So, is that the end?" the boy asked.

"No, not yet. For, you see, the people complained to the gods, and they prayed for some kind of divine intervention, for some god to come down and stop the good king who had turned bad, and finally another god heard them. He was a clever god, well known for disguising himself, and he thought it over. He couldn't break the deal the other god had made, and he seemed to be stuck, until he finally figured it out.

"This god waited until dusk, that time when it isn't quite day and it isn't quite night but in between, then the god turned himself into a beautiful girl and stood outside the king's palace and did a sexy dance."

"Jennifer Lopez?"

"Yeah, like that."

"In any case, she danced and danced and the king looked out the window and she was so enticing that the king got crazy to be with her. She crooked her finger for him to come closer, and he raced down the stairs and was going to run out into the courtyard to where she was when she put up her hand for him to stop. He halted in the doorway, both hands on the doorjambs, and he watched her do her sexy dance.

"All of a sudden there was a flash. The king was blinded, and Jennifer Lopez turned into a yellow tiger with long claws. And the tiger tore the flesh of the king with her nails, blood splattering indoors and out.

"The bad king was dead. It was dusk—it wasn't night and it wasn't day—and he was standing in the doorway—it wasn't indoors and it wasn't outdoors—and he was sliced up with the tiger's nails, no human weapon, so the god had honored the conditions set down by the first god who had granted the king's wish, and the people were glad.

"Pretty good story, huh?" The father patted the boy's head and began to get up. "Good night."

"Wait, Dad, that's it? That's the whole story? I don't get it."

"Well, I suppose the moral is 'Don't get a big head or treat people badly just because you think you're lucky or rich.' Or maybe, the moral is 'Be sure to read the fine print before you make any deal,'" the father chuckled, standing in the bedroom door.

"Maybe it means another thing," said the boy, his brow furrowed with worry.

"What else do you think?"

"Maybe the story means you should never stand in doorways."

TEN

Novelist

Only because he had lost something, although he didn't know what it was, did he write. He wrote in order to discover what he had lost—and then, once found, to lose it again.

Inspiration

The elderly gentleman opened the door. He looked excessively dignified in a tuxedo jacket, except that he wore no pants, not even underpants, and he sported a huge erection. He declared in a sonorous, cultured voice, "The Whore of Babylon will see you now."

Duty

I knew what Dad was after when he took the Bowie knife and drove up with me to Twin Peaks. He had gotten orders. He didn't like the orders. He was obliged to carry them out and I was obliged to cooperate. I thought of running away, but I knew that I could never escape the inevitability of such a monumental command, that I had a role to play and I was called upon to play it well. Besides, I felt sorry for him.

"Dad," I said, laying my head on a boulder and extending my neck. "Be brave."

Life

When he was young, he thought life would be one continuous screenplay with an exciting musical score. But when he reached middle age he realized it's more like a collage, a cutup, disconnected bits and pieces—not a novel but a commonplace book filled with phrases, amusing remarks, fuzzy memories. Actually, it's not even like a collage, since his life was more torn, more random, with no guiding consciousness at all—no artist, no editor, just bulldozers pushing odds and ends onto convenient, moldering piles of Elmer's Glue.

Art

All along she had thought that her art involved holding up a mirror to the world, to the traffic and bustle of the human comedy, the way Stendhal said, and suddenly she discovered that indeed she was holding up a mirror—except that it was facing the wrong way.

Guard

The guard would treat the prisoners with contempt and beat them from time to time, sending them to spend days, even months, in utter darkness. He put bugs in their food, abused them in all sorts of ways. But then she would, for no apparent reason, lay her hand gently on a prisoner's head, pat a shoulder, smile, offer a flicker of compassion, and in this way she made a discovery. Such unaccountable acts of kindness would unhinge the prisoners. Any inmate treated this way would have his will collapse in no time, and his sanity soon after. Perhaps it was because the guard was a woman, perhaps not. Some turned canine and became virtual slaves, willing to do anything just to receive a pat on the head or a slight smile. But others begged to be beaten and would howl in agony at any sign of affection. Given only crumbs, they preferred starvation, although the guard dispensed a steady, erratic diet of violence seasoned with gentle touches, which turned out to be the worst torture of all.

Nothing

One day he gazed into the mirror and saw that his nose actually hangs down to his chin, his left eye seems to be missing, his teeth are far too long and far too green, bright red blotches of skin sprout from his forehead, clumps of hair keep falling from his scalp, and he has a third eyebrow traveling down the center of his nose. It was not a pleasant sight. "And this," he said to the image in the glass, "is just the beginning."

Bar Code

"The ATM card and the Bar Code are digital monsters!" the minister exclaimed. "They know our names, assign us our numbers; they stamp our invisible accounts, drain the blood of our work; they discover the way we live, how we move, our secret desires—the all-seeing, all-knowing ATM card, the fiendish Bar Code. Behold the Mark of the Beast!"

The congregation gasped and moaned, calling for God's mercy.

Bob, a loan officer for Bank of America, was the single bank employee in the church, and he slumped forward in his pew, quietly sobbing.

Everywhere he went, it seemed, the Anti-Christ kept following him.

Mars Virus

They met her in a field hundreds of feet away from any building or intelligent road, their Genital Communicators disconnected, all implants disabled as much as possible. They were clear of all nanomechanical devices, all programming, all cybersomatic interfaces.

"Let's get to the point," they began. "You have had no implants, no enhancements, you are as digitally clean as someone from the era of smokestacks and locomotives, and we're speaking with you here because we're trying to keep you pure, away from any interface. It's because you are clean, that's why we need you."

Covenant

"How many circumcisions have you done, Rabbi?" the father asked.

"About six thousand."

"That's impressive."

The rabbi shrugged, but the father regarded him as a master. In his mind's eye he envisioned a cavalcade of tiny dicks, a lifetime of tiny dicks, each expertly clipped.

Soon it was time for the rabbi to go, and the father folded the cash for the *bris* in his palm.

"Be careful when you change his diaper not to pull off the bandage," he advised, then quickly departed, his little black case and *yarmulke* bobbing down the steps.

Everyone else left except for parents and child. After the first, brief moment of pain, the boy was the same self-possessed, calm, happy baby as before.

When it came time to change his diaper that evening, the mother rested in bed while the father put him on the changing table in his room. Gently, he undid the pins and slowly, carefully, he pulled the diaper off.

To his astonishment, blood spurted up at him. The bandage, stuck to the front of the diaper, had come off. Fumbling to put the bandage back on, he kept his mouth shut, panic rising in his throat.

He finally cried out, and she hastened over.

"Oh, my God! Quick, call the hospital!"

The hospital advised that they call the *mohel*. "He knows what he's doing."

He dialed the rabbi and described what had happened.

"Is he bleeding?"

"A lot. I don't know what happened."

The rabbi said he would be right over. The fact that his voice cracked did not reassure the father.

The father held a fresh diaper on his son's penis as the baby howled, the mother sobbing in the bedroom. He held back tears as the diaper stained red.

He had killed his own son. He had let a witch doctor slice him. The boy was being cursed with his father's sins. It was the Evil Eye. He had married out of the faith. He had refused to move to Israel. Any number of self-accusations crossed his mind, and while they would flit away in an instant, each recrimination left its residue of uncertainty and suspicion.

Soon the rabbi came to the door, rushing up the steps to the bedroom. He glanced quickly at the blood-spurting penis and nervously opened his black bag. The mother sobbed and wept, the boy howled, and the father stood to the rabbi's side, shaking. Once again, the rabbi's experienced, steady hands wrapped gauze around the wound, although the father did notice beads of perspiration gathering on his forehead as he worked. But the bandage wouldn't stay, and blood kept flowing. Steadily, the rabbi cut a second piece of gauze, and this time he succeeded. The bleeding stopped, and he wrapped a fresh diaper over the new bandage.

"It's alright. The boy's fine," he said, handing the baby over to his tearful mother and then wiping his forehead with a handkerchief.

"What happened?" the father, still trembling, asked. "Why did this happen?"

The rabbi packed up his case, his own hands quivering slightly, although he maintained his professional self-control.

"His penis withdrew inside of him like a turtle. And when it did, the bandage came off. Sometimes this happens, the penis pulling in afterwards. Unusual, but natural."

The father instantly recognized what he had described. Sometimes his own penis would withdraw or retract, a little quirk, no big deal. Only later did it occur to him that the curse he feared was cast on his son may have been his own DNA.

"How many times have you seen this happen?"

His case snapped shut, the rabbi hastened out of the bedroom, back down the steps and out the door. He acted as if he had many appointments to keep—or he was too shook up to linger.

"How many times?" the father repeated.

"I've seen this happen about three times, I think."

Quickly, the father calculated six thousand circumcisions divided by three quirks—one time for each two thousand.

"That's not very often," he called out, as the rabbi rushed out to the sidewalk.

"A little unusual, but natural," he repeated, sliding behind the steering wheel of his old Chevrolet.

He held the key in the ignition and glanced up at the father. "Not to worry."

Then the *mohel* slammed the door shut and tore off, burning rubber.

Instructions for Reading

Unlike in the movies, there are certain things in life you cannot edit out, things that ought to be erased but stubbornly remain, taking a drink in a sleazy bar, hiding boogers under your desk in first grade, bad jokes, dirty diapers, car payments—petty items that should be irrelevant to your main story line, yet they persist, ambient sounds, chores, habits, bodily functions, annoyances, trivial amusements, receipts, static—they all grow huge, overwhelming everything else, filling up the deep pit of remembrance, clogging the toilet.

Insane

Out on the street, children not much younger than the militiaman scurried and played, families went in and out of the apartment building that abutted no-man's-land, a one-block field of rubble marking the division between East and West Beirut. The militiaman was from one of the smaller leftist groups in the nationalist front. Just a teenager, he smiled at us from underneath the tent of the checkpoint that was dug out of a basement below street level. Across the lot rose another apartment building, its walls blown out to reveal a skeleton of floors and walls. On its fifth floor, behind sandbags, perched a Falangist unit.

The militiaman introduced us to one of the neighborhood men, who brought me and my Palestinian guide, a cadre from the Popular Front, inside to share the customary round of coffee. His living-room wall was cracked but intact, significant because the outer wall faced regular firefights across the field of rubble. They would take cover, but they had gotten used to it. He shrugged. The line of confrontation had stayed the same for years, so things seemed as normal as they could get, considering.

Seemingly unaware of danger, kids squealed in play behind the large earthen embankment pushed up to barricade the street and shield it from sniper fire.

I peeked around the side of the barricade and was surprised to see a single man, middle-aged and grizzled, wearing pajamas and weaving through no-man's-land, loudly singing off-key. I looked up at the Falangist position, afraid that a shot would in a moment tear the howling drunk to pieces. No one stirred on the other side. The man stumbled around in the rubble, an easy target, and I watched nervously as he meandered over to our side and slipped around the earthwork. He saw me, an obvious foreigner, and stopped in his tracks, reeking of alcohol. He glared and pointed, then laughed and bellowed out a song more growl than melody, before pushing off down the crowded street.

He was the neighborhood crazy man, the militiaman explained, and he wandered where he liked, doing pretty much as he pleased, unharmed by either side. In the Arab world there is a tradition to honor madmen as people infused with a kind of divine inspiration, and so babblers and raving drunks are tolerated, even cared for, as special tokens of holiness. And so this happy drunk could fearlessly zigzag across no-man's-land, a true noncombatant, free to come and go as he pleased. How mad could he really be to have figured out a way to survive the violent demarcations of the civil war?

The Falangist position in the building on the other side appeared to consist of three or so soldiers idling around, looking like they were playing cards. I moved around the side of the earthwork, took a step into no-man's-land, and raised my camera to take a picture of the unit. I screwed the lens around to focus and as the blur of shadows and glinting cement on the fifth floor became clear through the viewfinder, I discerned one of the Falangists, his rifle raised, taking his own bead on me.

For a brief moment we locked in on each other's sights.

"Get down!" my guide yelled. He tackled me to the ground, just as the bullet exploded past my head.

Only the city I am about to leave is holy.

Art

Thumb through the History of Art and eventually you will come upon an Italian Renaissance painting of an old man, a grandfather looking down at his grandson in his arms, "An Old Man and His Grandson" by some artist named Ghirardelli Chocolate or something, I can't remember. The boy has curly blonde hair and a small brimless cap, the kind Chico Marx might wear, and his soft little hand reaches to hold his grandfather's cloak as he looks up sweetly into the old man's eyes. In the background, above the boy's head, there's a window, and through it I can see a road snaking around, spotted with perfectly conical trees, a hill up close with more scraggly trees, and further back a steep mountain jutting straight up from flatland, like the mountain in *Close Encounters of the Third Kind*. What a dreamy, make-believe place awaits us outside that window—although the real focus of the painting is on the old man, especially his nose.

The old man smiles gently, his expression tender, loving, and slightly sad, his gray hair swept back, his eyes almost shut as he looks down, basking in the light of the boy's sweet face, the old man's gaze deeply satisfied. But I am drawn to the grandfather's nose like a moth to flame; nothing else can hold my eye. That nose is astonishing. It's redder and more bulbous than the shnozolas of W. C. Fields or Jimmy Durante, and it's cracked and covered with hideous growths. But the boy doesn't seem to notice it, as he lovingly beams up at the old man—or maybe he does notice it and he's not really looking at the old man's face but up his nostrils, marveling at the monstrosity. Perhaps he's accustomed to the freakishness and love has smoothed out all the rosy welts, or it's so familiar that he's not just grown comfortable but even enjoys the sight, like the way I used to wait for my grandmother to pull out her false teeth and fall asleep with her head thrown back and her jaw open so I could peer into the creepy, dark, ruby cavern of her mouth.

But I can't turn my eyes away from that nose, and I can't figure out what's going on. There's something so real, so vivid, so incredibly ugly about the nose, that my fascination is obsessive, and I can only imagine that everyone who's seen the picture for the last 400 years or so has felt the same.

The artist must be trying to say something—but what?

He bowed his head, offering his father's dung.
"La Vida Loca!" the Santo Niño sung.

Ritual

Every year Aaron made a point of watching his video-tape of Charlie Chaplin's *Modern Times*, and every year he would cry. No lack of funny stuff, but somehow the movie always put him in some sort of dreamy, melancholic rever-ie. Sadness suffused every shot, including the laughers, and those scenes that are supposed to be touching, even maudlin, worked into his heart like a Texan drilling for oil. Even before the end of the opening montage—a herd of sheep dissolving into a crowd of jostling proletarians on their way to work—he would be reduced to tears. And that brilliant opening sequence of the Little Tramp driven to insanity on the assembly line would move him to guffaws and sobs.

With every viewing he would fish out something new about the film, a nuance or an insight he had never noticed before. He would be astonished that still, after so many years, he could discover yet another marvel, and Aaron would stop the tape, rewind, pause, and examine the detail or the composition of the frame with tumultuous delight. There was the time, long ago, that he finally noticed that the large woman Charlie bumps against in the crowded paddy-wagon is actually Black, and as he keeps on getting thrown against her she shoves the little white man back. It was a sly, even subliminal, gesture to include an uppity Black woman in the 1930s, no matter how briefly, and he felt a pang of poignancy at the revelation.

Aaron spent several years pondering the automatic feeding-machine in the assembly-line sequence. He noticed how stiff and mechanical, even prim and proper, the machine behaves during the trial run with Charlie strapped in before the circular feeding table, and even when the contraption goes berserk and dispenses chaos and destruction instead of lunch, the machine maintains its sense of injured dignity. After each assault, the automatic face-wiper, with great daintiness, rolls slowly, majestically, politely, back and forth across his lips like a blotter in the hands of an elegant butler, and Aaron realized that the machine is just a counterpart of Charlie, is itself a gentleman reduced to play its sad role in the universe, just like the Tramp, and the intersection of human and machine, violence and courtesy, seemed a bittersweet *pas de deux* that brought—once again—tears to Aaron's eyes.

This year he stopped at the scene where Charlie, spending a surreptitious night with the Gamin in the department store where he works as night watchman, goes on a roller-skating spree. To entertain his love, he ties a blindfold around his eyes and skates around a balcony floor, not realizing that it is under construction and that the railing has been removed. One false step and he will fly off the balcony to disaster or even death. But with the blindfold on he skates with effortless grace, blissfully unaware of the danger, skirting the very edge of doom, prancing with his cane. Not knowing of the abyss, he twirls and swivels, the very embodiment of virtuoso ease, the girl's eyes wide in horror. But when finally he yanks off the blindfold and beholds the great danger, his legs turn to rubber, he loses balance, he flails his arms, he teeters in a panic on the edge. The Tramp finally crawls away on all fours, his skill and grace stolen from him with the sudden advent of vision.

"His blindness is his virtue," Aaron mused. "The Great Man masters the brink by not knowing it, while mere mortals open their eyes and plunge to their doom."

He began to cry.

The artist's wager is to save chaos from order.

Instructions for Living

"Live every day as if it were your last, the day you die, and then all your days will be filled with worthy deeds and deep thoughts." So writes the emperor in his meditations. For Marcus Aurelius this might be good advice, but Steve realized that it would not do for him, since he was more slave than emperor. So he wrote in his own journal, "Live every day as if it were *the day before you are born*. This way nothing makes sense, deeds can hardly be worthy, thoughts have not yet formed, much less become deep, and death is just more of the same." What a relief.

Facts are Signs of natural Words.

Signs are real, vivid, and incredibly ugly.

Facts and Signs lock into each other's sights.

Words indicate who crosses the threshold first.

What a relief.

Delete.

"Be Back in Five Minutes," said the bombardier.

Satan's Asshole

"You were standing along a hillside, maybe even this one, and a man with a ski mask held a gun to your head and he spouted off some crazy talk, something about Dante and hell. That's all I could see. And then I couldn't see him anymore, he was gone, it was like he just sank into the ground or something."

"That's what you saw?" Danny DeVito stammered to the coed called Prophetic Attractions.

"Yeah, I thought maybe it was a movie I saw through clairvoyance—but one that was never released, you know? Maybe it was just some script. Do you know anything about it?"

She waited, wondering if the movie star would confirm her vision.

He said nothing for a long time.

"Maybe the idea would work as a movie, you know, but I don't know of any movie like that, even one that wasn't released," he said, finally. "And I've never worked in such a film myself."

"How strange," she said.

He apologized that he couldn't be more helpful.

"Well, maybe it was just a dream, some nutty daydream, and I'm glad," Prophetic Attractions told the two actors, smiling. "Seeing all these films, you know, having this power, I mean, it was just kind of too much, so I'm glad."

"We're glad, too," Rhea Perlman said. "We're glad you're relieved."

"Somehow she saw what happened, didn't she?" Danny whispered, as she left, a smile fixed on his face. "She saw just as clearly as that woman who ended up wrecking her car and getting amnesia. Rhea, what's going on?"

"I don't know, I really don't know," Rhea muttered, waving at the car as it turned down the long driveway.

Suddenly, Danny looked down, startled. He saw that he was up to his ankles in the Malibu mud, and he began to sink down deeper and deeper by the second.

"My God, now it's happening to me!"

Christine's Son

Her father always cruelly toyed with Christine's emotions, promising to visit or take her to Disneyland but never coming through, or coming through so erratically that she learned not to expect anything of him, except, of course, that she always did, and when she would go to his house every other weekend according to the court order he would ply her with dresses and gifts and candy, which would only make her angry when she returned to her mother's house, and she would throw herself into tantrums as a consequence, dark clouds over her head for days, punishment for his ex-wife that her father greatly desired, no doubt. After years of getting batted around and manipulated, Christine grew cynical and insecure, and as soon as she reached puberty she zeroed in on boys, became obsessed, and for years she was hardly a day without a boyfriend, always stuffing their penises into the hollowness of her soul, although she wasn't a slut, didn't grab boys off the street or anything, just that she always needed a boy, one she could control, could insist upon staying put, could fill her emptiness, until they couldn't stand it anymore and one by one the boys would flee, only to be replaced in a matter of days by another. She went on like this, chewing up and spitting out boyfriends one after the other, until one day she announced that she was pregnant, and rather than being horrified to carry a child at such a young age she was pleased and radiated a sublime joy that could only be regarded as crazy foolishness by her mother.

But when she gave birth to her son, she continued to glow, and she seemed changed, no longer needing a boyfriend, at least not in the same way. She had been fulfilled, calmed, and centered—she had been made whole by the little boy. Weird as it may seem, when Christine gave birth to her son it was as if she had actually given birth to her own father, and once she could suckle and raise her own father, once she could devote herself to the little father, and he to her, once fear and domination and insecurity transformed into a mother's love, she became herself.

Out of the closet and into the streets

Over and out

Out of bounds

Bound for glory

Outside chance

Out at first

First Things First

Who's on First

Time Out

Prisoner

The cell was so completely dark, so dense, that he learned to discern depths of blackness instead of shapes and surfaces. He could smell the walls and he could feel them as well. As his hands climbed to the low ceiling, each crack or texture in the cement began to be filled with tactile meanings. Familiar bumps gave him comfort, while the rough surface near the floor seemed to speak of remorse, and the smoothness at shoulder level of serenity.

The cell was totally, eerily silent, as well. Gone were the incessant screams and hollers from the main cellblock, which was a relief, but the deep silence was so impenetrable he could barely stand it. Talking or humming to himself would give his tormentors more than he desired, so he kept quiet, although every morning he did make a point of bellowing out songs—Broadway show tunes, hymns, Beatles—for fifteen minutes, or what seemed to be fifteen minutes, before doing his pushups and other exercises. This way his guards would know that his silence was a form of discipline, that it was purposeful, as much as his raucous vocals and deep-knee bends.

Then he discovered that he could hear himself breathe. In and out, it was like wind in trees or the mild rush of a creek. He could sit and listen to himself breathe for hours, it seemed, and it calmed him as his concentration delved deeper into his being. He had never practiced meditation before, but now he found that simply listening to the rush of his lungs was a kind of sweetness not to be missed, and he could listen for hours at a time, could feel the thickness of his soul, and what seemed at first to be the darkness of his insides was actually a bright light-filled cosmos. In all the gloom he had actually found illumination, and the fact that he had swindled his tormentors made him smile.

Also important was the discovery of his fingers. When he held them closely to his ear and rubbed one finger against his thumb, a kind of rough, loud whisper filled his ears. Each finger took on a personality. Rubbing thumb and index finger was the Mama, middle finger of course was the Papa, fourth finger the older son, while the pinky—hard to pull over to the thumb—was the small-voiced baby girl. Left hand and right, he would hold the fingers to his ears and rub, and though nothing could be heard an inch or two away, up close whole conversations between the two families would chatter away. This meant his narrow cell was actually filled with a great deal of company, and each day there would be a new episode in the adventures of Left Hand and Right, his own intimate puppet show.

Inner light, families of fingers, Braille-like walls—in this way he did not grow weary or go insane. Then, one day, the door opened, and another prisoner was shoved in to share the tiny cell with him, and everything changed.

HILTON OBENZINGER

A wrongful life lawsuit
allows a child to sue its parents
by making the claim

that it would rather not have been born
and the parents were negligent
in not preventing its birth.

Artist

About the time Britney Spears topped the charts, he began to notice that young women were wearing shirts that seemed to have shrunk in the wash, exposing tummies and belly buttons to the light of day. As a sculptor he prided himself on his eye for mass quirks, so when he gave it some thought he realized that the fashion had actually been around for quite some time before the nubile singer had exclaimed, *"I'm not that innocent!"* Most erotic poses are better performed in the dark, at special times and in special places, but bare midriffs did seem innocent, a kind of daytime, nonchalant sexiness, available for breakfast, lunch, or dinner, and perhaps not *that* innocent either.

Cropped tops the blouses were called, and he considered the notion of cropping tops intriguing. That's when he got the idea for his series of pieces, "Midriff Crops," like a sequence of busts. At first they were torsos—trunks with no arms, no legs, no heads—but eventually he cropped that even further, producing only midsections from the bottom curvature of the breasts to just above the groin. Cropped blouses and bellies and navels carved or molded in marble or plastic or clay or plaster of Paris. One by one he built up his series, midriffs of all variations—he hadn't realized all the nuances, the dramatic and comic theatrics, to which the exposed tummy lent itself—and he was pleased. So too were the critics.

All went well until the day he arrived at his studio to find a phalanx of police there. A neighbor had discovered something hideous in a plastic bag outside his door—a female torso, nothing but a torso, wearing a blouse with an exposed midriff, the body hacked cleanly at the breasts and at the groin.

The police wanted to ask him some questions. "This—this is someone's daughter," he gasped in horror. "How could someone do this?"

"Maybe the perpetrator wanted to be an artist," replied the detective with a curious look, "like you."

Dear Boy,

After the graduation ceremony, the woman came up to me in the large room that served as both cafeteria and gym. She wore a basket on her head, and the thick tattooed lines that worked from the edges of her mouth down her chin in the traditional Yurok fashion signaled that she was part of the cultural revival that had started around the time of Alcatraz—you know, the Indian occupation?—which was when I was a teacher there. She introduced herself as the school board member from that part of the river, and said, "Brad

Honeysuckle just told me he and his
brothers were so bad that they drove
you out and you never taught school
again. Is that true?" There they were,
twenty-five years later, the
Honeysuckle boys still doing mischief,
and I laughed. "No, I did teach after
I left, although that's not all I've
done," I told her. "I've been a print-
er, among other things, and I teach
now, at Stanford, so that's really not
true." And she hastened back over to
the crowd gossiping around the cup-
cakes to nip Brad Honeysuckle's rumor
in the bud.

But I didn't mind Brad Honeysuckle's
little tease. The day before, the
school held a fundraising bingo game.
I bought several cards just to make a
donation and chatted with the old
school cook. You know I never win anything, which is why I never play the
lottery, but this time, to my astonishment, one of my cards actually hit
Bingo. Well, that was amazing enough
and I expected maybe a berry pie or
some deer jerky. But I had won one of
the big prizes, which was a swaddling
basket for a baby, just a small-sized
basket, more for a doll and not one
you would really use for a baby, but
still a real piece of Yurok weaving,
and I was pleased no end.

I was even more pleased to discover
that the weaver of the basket was none
other than Mrs. Honeysuckle herself,
the mother of Brad and his brothers.
Oh, we had so many hard times, and she
had so many visits to the twenty-two-
year-old principal's office. I even
had to testify in court, those boys
were just so wild, and she stuck by
them no matter what. They weren't
really mean and we always patched
things up, at least enough to keep
things afloat. So you could just imagine how amazed I was that after so
many years, not only did I win a
prize, but I won a basket made by the
mother of the most difficult, trouble-
some boys in the school.

I chuckled at this, and as I walked
out after the bingo game to put the
swaddling basket in my car, I saw Mrs.
Honeysuckle, thanked her for the basket, which was really beautiful, and
asked about her kids. It turned out
Brad's daughter was one of the eighth-
graders graduating the next day, while
Ben was running for tribal council, so
they were fine, and we parted. It was
as if she had one more meeting with
the principal, but this time there was
peace.

I was alone outside the school, which
looked almost exactly the same as it

did years before, and I absent-minded-
ly strolled around. Then something
caught my eye by the side of the
school bus garage. I saw a bright red
feather, a single feather, dancing on
top of a bush, and I picked it up. I
hadn't noticed any red birds, but
there was this red feather, and I had
been around Indians long enough, not
just Yuroks but others, to know that
this red feather, and the fact that I
had found it right then, meant something. I couldn't really tell what it
meant, if it was good or bad, and I
didn't even know what kind of bird it
came from, but I felt that it must be
a good sign, and that it gave some
kind of power to the basket when I
slid it inside the weave, placing the
red feather where the child's head
would rest.

I put the basket with the feather in
my car and suddenly felt tremendously
sleepy, like I was drugged. So I put
myself behind the steering wheel of
the rented car, tilted the seat back,
and dropped off to deep Rip Van Winkle
sleep almost immediately.

It seemed that in no time I began to
dream. In my dream I was fishing along
the gravel bar down on the Klamath
near the Honeysuckle place and as
usual I couldn't fish worth a damn,

humiliating myself as always with my ineptitude. I tried to cast my line, whipping the rod behind me and only ended up tangling myself in the string, the hook grabbing me by my shoulder, just the same as when I had tried twenty-five years before. The more I worked to untangle myself the more the line circled and snarled up, until finally I yanked one last time, and ended up flinging myself into the water headfirst. I was quickly caught in the swift current, tumbling head over heels down the Klamath.

Big steelhead salmon and sturgeon and eels and other fish came up to me, examined this bundle of struggling string, and swam off, their curiosity satisfied. I would stare into their blank eyes, peering deeply into the strange, imponderable phantoms of the river. I wasn't scared and I wasn't drowning, although I was deep underwater. I just kept on reeling in the fishing line. I realized that I had also caught it in the line and I was reeling it in along with myself. It was like I was fishing for myself and I was a big catch, if I could only haul myself in, but I was also reeling in the basket, which was maybe an even bigger catch, although I had no way to choose. I twirled the reel and tumbled

in the line, one summersault after
another, and the basket whizzed around
and around as well, until suddenly I
gave the line one last jerk, and in an
instant found myself back on the gravel bar, free of all the tangled fishing line, dripping wet but glad.
Beside me was the basket, safe and
sound as well, but now inside of it
there was a little baby boy, wrapped
up tightly in a giant red feather like
a swaddling blanket, his feet snug
inside, and he was laughing at me and
my troubles. That's when I woke up.

All of this seemed significant, even
the fact that after I woke up from the
dream I was so dazed that I stumbled
out and ended up slamming the door
behind me and locking the key in the
car. I couldn't believe it. The school
bus driver had to jimmy the door open
for me—once again the bumbling school-
teacher needed help—and I figured that
must mean something too.

Either every little thing was a sign
or nothing was. Clearly, I was a fool,
and if I was going to save myself, and
even more important, if I was going to
save a little boy, then I had to
become a fool in the river and not out
of it, and I had to reel myself in.
But whether the boy was you or me or a
baby Moses or Brad Honeysuckle, who

could tell? Even with dreams I bum-
bled. I had a good one, a dream heaped
with meaning, yet I couldn't really
figure it out, and I had to live with
it, tumbling in the river, snarling
myself up again and again, grasping at
hints.

So when that lady with the chin tattoos from the school board came up to
me with Brad Honeysuckle's wisecrack,
I had to chuckle, and I knew the
Honeysuckle brothers were just big,
laughing fish sniffing curiously at
the creature knotted up with his own
line. I had received real gifts—the
basket, the feather, and the dream—and
after twenty-five years I had become
foolish enough to haul in my heart and
my soul, and that was a pretty good
catch for the Klamath, even if I never
understand a damn thing.

Adieu

This, then, is where our story begins.

Christine's Mom

All the kids are grown up now, but every time they come
over to eat roast beef or turkey or baked ham, Christine's

Mama would remember "The Patty Hearst Roast Beef," and they would all sigh and then laugh.

The SLA made its demand for the food giveaway, and when it came time for the poor to collect their bags of groceries, Mama went right down to Glide Church and stood in line, took her bag from Reverend Cecil Williams like all the rest. The SLA may have been extremists, but that didn't matter. After all, she had three kids and was on welfare and could use the food and the Hearst family was giving it away, anyway, and long ago she had put feeding her kids way ahead of any scruples.

The bag had milk and bread and other goods, but most of all it had a huge hunk of beef, which she immediately slipped into the oven. When she put it on the table their eyes almost bugged out, it was so big. But when they tore into it, they were in heaven. Never had they tasted meat as tender, as delicious. Like the saying goes, it melted in your mouth, you could cut it like butter, it was that succulent. Meat was expensive, hard to come by on welfare, although once in a while they had pork chops mixed in with tons of macaroni and gov'mint cheese. But this—this was some kind of gourmet deluxe cut oozing with flavor and juices, a roast beef none of them ever imagined could exist.

Year after year Mama would invariably recall "The Patty Hearst Roast Beef" at Thanksgiving or someone's birthday, even though she's long off welfare. It was one of those rituals that marked the years, like saying grace. Her eyes would cloud over, she would get dreamy and drift off to the memory of that wonderful gift and a different time. Then she would sigh, and her children would all burst out laughing at the idea of becoming nostalgic for a hunk of meat.

"Thank you, Patty Hearst," Mama would say, in a kind of grace, and they would scream out in response, "THANK YOU PATTY HEARST ROAST BEEF," and laugh some more, and they would then dig in and grub out.

EPILOGUE

When the boy came back we were amazed and cried with joy. Where had he been? What had happened? But he refused to answer. We cajoled, we threatened, we pleaded, but the most he would say was that he didn't know except that everything had been dark and he couldn't see, although it was very clear that he was lying.

We were too happy to care at first and then it didn't seem to matter. We would linger by his bedroom door, and listen to him in his fitful sleep. We held back from waking him, and he would mutter strange things like "Danny DeVito" and "Hasta la vista, Baby." We just sighed and looked at each other. Had he spent all that time at the movies?

Eventually, we had to accept the fact that a mystery like a chasm had opened up in the center of his being, somewhere between West End Avenue and Broadway. If we were lucky, he would never fall into that hole again.

But if we weren't careful, if we inadvertently stumbled over the edge, if we opened a trap door we never knew existed, he would once again plunge into the depths, never to return.

Hilton Obenzinger's books include *Running Through Fire: How I Survived the Holocaust by Zosia Goldberg as told to Hilton Obenzinger*, an oral history of his aunt's ordeal during the war; *American Palestine: Melville, Twain, and the Holy Land Mania*, a literary and historical study of America's fascination with the Holy Land; *Cannibal Eliot and the Lost Histories of San Francisco*, a novel of invented documents that recounts the history of San Francisco from the Spanish conquest to the 1906 earthquake and fire; *New York on Fire*, a history of the fires of New York in verse, selected by the *Village Voice* as one of the best books of the year and nominated by the Bay Area Book Reviewer's Association for its poetry award; and *This Passover Or The Next I Will Never Be in Jerusalem*, winner of the Before Columbus American Book Award.

Born in 1947 in Brooklyn, raised in Queens, and graduating Columbia College in 1969, he has taught on the Yurok Indian Reservation, operated a community printing press in San Francisco's Mission District, co-edited a publication devoted to Middle East peace, and worked as a commercial writer and instructional designer. He received his doctorate in the Modern Thought and Literature Program at Stanford University in 1997 and currently teaches writing and American literature at Stanford.